THE PROBLEM WITH PUGS

A Love & Pets Romantic Comedy, Book 1

A. G. HENLEY

CENTRAL PARK BOOKS

Text copyright © 2018 by A.G. Henley

Cover Designed by Najla Qamber Designs (www.najlaqamberdesigns.com)

Formatting by L. M. Perkins

Visit me at aghenley.com

Summary: When a young woman's boyfriend breaks up with her and leaves her their dog, she must help the dog adjust to new men in her life.

For all pet lovers and readers.
You know who you are.

CONTENTS

Hey, readers!

Get the FREE prequel ebook to the Love & Pets series, *Love, Pugs, and Other Problems,* an exclusive short story that tells how Amelia gets Doug the pug instead of a ring!

Chapter One

On the one hundred and third day since Tim left, the frantic call comes in.

I'm walking home from work. The streets of LoDo, Lower Downtown Denver, Colorado, are warm and buzzy, like a beer after a summer hike. It's only four thirty in the afternoon, but for once, I didn't have to sneak out. The partners at the law offices of Hart, Hand, & Butz had already left for the weekend.

I wind around the stream of baseball fans in grape-colored Rockies gear headed toward Coors Field. Vendors hawk dollar bottles of water and bags of peanuts, and parking attendants direct cars with purple pennants.

The fans walk fast, excited to get to the game. I'm excited to get home, put on pj's, snuggle with Doug, and wait. Friday is Tim's night to video call, which means it's the best night of our week. A few minutes, and I'd be there.

"Spare some change?" A man asks from his seat on the sidewalk. He has scruffy, sandy hair, a beard with chewing gum stuck in it, and dirt-stained jeans. He also has a dog with him, some kind of terrier mutt with the same sandy, scruffy hair as the man.

I dig in my tote for my wallet, accidentally dumping my makeup bag, keys, and completely unnecessary birth control pill pack on the ground in front of him. He helps gather them up while I find a five-dollar bill. I trade him for my stuff.

"Will this help?" I ask.

"Ten would help more." His smile is cheeky.

"I'm so sorry, that's all the cash I have." I peer in my bag. "Would you like half a turkey sandwich?"

"Got any roast beef in there? Roast beef is Sparky's favorite."

The dog barks and wags its tail. I shake my head.

"Then we'll take the turkey," he says.

I sigh as I walk on. I can't get anything right this week, even helping the homeless. But I definitely couldn't pass the man by— or his dog.

A few blocks later, my goal is in sight: the top of our apartment building. Thank God. My phone rings, but it's a number I don't recognize.

"Hello?" I answer.

"Avery?"

I can't place the man's accented voice at first. "No, this is her sister, Amelia."

"Ah, Amelia! Come quick . . ." He says something in Spanish that I don't catch.

I hear a growl and several sharp barks alarmingly close to the phone.

"Manuel? Is that you?" I walk faster.

"*Sí!* I come to your apartment to fix *el baño*, but *el perro*—"

"I'll be right there!" I hang up, toss my phone in my bag, and jog as best I can in four-inch heels. What has Doug done now?

Skirt flapping against my thighs, I hurry down the street, jaywalk between two cars, and yank open the glass doors to the lobby of the building before ducking into the elevator. Manuel's office door is ajar. He's not inside.

I tap my hand against my leg while the car slow-motions to the tenth floor. The doors open, and I wobble down to number 1001. The key trembles in my hand, and it takes me two tries to slide it in the lock. I turn the handle and rush in.

Light beams through the sliding glass door across the living room, blinding me. I drop my bag and throw my hand up to block it. The apartment is quiet.

As my eyes adjust, I can tell something horrible has happened. The chocolate-brown sofa pillows are thrown around, shredded and frosted with mounds of snowy feathers. A roll of toilet paper spools across the floor, and a few books splay open under the lower levels of the bookshelves, their pages torn. A leg of the coffee table is crooked.

Then I see them: two pairs of my most favorite underwear, crotches chewed.

The room looks like a slasher movie, post-slash.

"Manuel?" I call out.

"Amelia!" His voice is muffled. He sounds like he's in the master bedroom, but I'm not sure. Whatever he says next is drowned out by high-pitched, vicious barking.

I kick off my heels and charge around the corner to the bedroom hallway. At the end of it, the door to the master is closed. And standing guard in front is Doug.

He faces the door, sharp white teeth bared, tan-and-black fur standing in a ridge along his back. He's growling, and every time he barks, his tiny front feet shoot off the ground. His wrinkled and smushed black head is laser-focused on the shut door.

"Doug! What are you doing?"

Startled, he turns and rushes toward me, barking. For a second, I shy away and eye my own room. I could jump inside and slam the door.

What am I thinking? It's Doug—the sweet, adorable pug I share with Tim.

Instead of running, I drop to one knee and hold out my hands. "Dougie?"

Growling, he glares at the master door, then at me, then at the door again.

"Hold on, Manuel," I call. "I've almost got him."

"Lil' Dougie, come here." I slide closer, still wary, and touch his back. His head whips around. His eyes look glazed.

"C'mon, Doug. Let it go." I reach under his body and lift him up. He's rigid, still focused on the door, but he doesn't try to escape my hold. I hurry to my room, pop him in his crate, and shut my door on his feverish barking.

"Amelia?" Manuel calls.

"Coming!" I rush back into the hallway.

Our building manager peeks out of the master. His dark eyes dart around the floor, then find me. His normally sweet smile is nowhere to be seen as he creeps out, a wrench in hand.

"Did he bite you? Are you hurt?" I ask.

The hand holding the wrench relaxes. "No."

"What happened?"

"I came to fix the toilet. As soon as I pass the door"—he points the wrench accusingly at my bedroom, where Doug is still flipping out—"he attacked. He chase me down the hall, in there." The wrench points back at Avery's room. "I shut *el puerto* just in time and did the work. But when I finished, he won't let me out. He bite my boot."

He lifts up one of his heavy black work boots. Doug couldn't have done much damage to those, but still, my heart skips a beat. If he'd aimed higher, he could have really hurt him.

Manuel got us special permission to have Doug in the apartment back in March because Avery and her boyfriend Jason are such good tenants. And because I begged. If he wants to, he can kick Doug and me out on the street any time. I touch his tattooed arm.

"I'm so sorry about this, Manuel. I feel terrible that he scared you like that."

After a second, he nods. But he throws the stink eye at Doug through my door as he passes. I walk him out, apologizing all the way.

Doug quit barking as soon as the front door closed behind Manuel. Now he's whining. I ignore him as I right the books and the coffee-table leg, wind up the toilet paper roll and stick it under the bathroom sink, toss my underwear in the trash, and shove as much filling back into the sofa pillows as I can. Not much I can do about the corners Doug ripped out of them.

When the living room looks as good as it's going to, I pick my way across my messy bedroom and sit in front of the crate.

"Doug. You were a really bad boy today." I use my sternest voice.

He sits on his squishy butt, head down. His pink belly and fuzzy man parts show between his front legs. Slightly off-center dark eyes roll up toward me, silently begging for forgiveness.

"Why did you attack Manuel? He's always so nice to you when we see him."

Doug yips, and his tongue lolls out. I feel terrible that he trapped Manuel, tried to attack him, and destroyed the living room, but clearly *Doug* thinks he was doing his job.

After a minute, I relent and let him out. He launches himself at me, front paws on my chest. Laughing, I throw my head back while he tries to lick all over my face.

When I hear the front door open again, I put a finger in front of my mouth and shush him.

Avery and Jason's voices roll through the quiet apartment for a moment, then suddenly stop. Avery swears and Jason snickers.

"Amelia! Are you here?" My sister's voice is strained.

"Now what?" I ask Doug. He creeps back toward his crate, but I hold on to him and stand. "No way. I'm not facing the music alone." Why can't Tim call right now?

I stamp a smile on my face and walk out. They stand in the dining area, staring through the passage to the small kitchen. I can't see what they're looking at.

"Hey. What's going on?"

Avery's arms are crossed. She tilts her head. "Go on, see for yourself."

I peek in. I hadn't checked the kitchen while trying to cover up the destruction of the living room. Now that I see it, my hand flies to my mouth and I gasp in horror. On the ground next to the refrigerator is a torn bag of Starbucks's finest. Coffee grounds spill out, but most of the bag is gone.

"Doug must be high as a kite." Jason's dark eyes are amused. My sister's hazel ones look far from it.

I close my eyes and hold my pug tightly. He *is* squirming more than usual. Maybe the coffee was why he went after Manuel like that?

"Dougie?" I turn him so I can look at his eyes, although I'm not sure what I'm looking for. Do his pupils look larger than usual? "Are you okay?"

"He's not a baby, Amelia," Avery says. "He's a damn dog."

As if to prove her point, Doug wiggles enough that I have to let him go. He shakes himself and lifts his leg on a dining table chair.

"Doug, no!" I lunge at him, but it's too late. "I'm sorry, Avery, I just got home and haven't had a chance to take him out yet. I'll go now."

While Jason shakes with silent laughter, my sister's fair skin turns bright red. I scoop Doug up, clip his leash to his collar, and rush to the door, Avery's voice ringing in my ears: "And what happened to my couch pillows?"

I lean against the front door when it closes and shut my eyes. If Doug and I get kicked out, will the homeless man and his roast-beef loving dog show us the ropes on the street?

Chapter Two

Starbucks strikes, and Doug poops three times in the middle of the sidewalk. He always poops in the middle of the sidewalk—always—so it's impossible to pretend I don't notice and hurry off without picking it up like I see other dog owners doing. Of course I only have two bags to clean it up. I have to nudge the third turd into the grass with the toe of my shoe before we slink back to the apartment.

Avery and Jason sit on the sofa. She's holding one of the mutilated cushions in her hands, and a rag sits under the table leg where Doug peed, soaking it up.

I grab the pet-stain spray from the kitchen and start cleaning. "Aves, I'm really sorry. Something got into him today."

"Yeah. Half a bag of French roast." Jason chortles.

Guilt surges through me. I think I left a partially unpacked grocery tote of pantry items—including that bag of coffee—on the floor last night.

Doug trots out through the open sliding door to the small balcony. He alternates between barking his head off and chewing on one of Tim's old T-shirts that I knotted up for him a few months ago. I lost Doug's favorite stuffed cat, Catticus, in the move here, and he won't touch any of the new toys I bought him to play with.

I finish the mop job, perch on the edge of a chair, and sneak a glance at my watch. Fifteen minutes until Tim's call.

"Good thing it wasn't a bag of weed," Jason says. "You might have come home to him belly-up on the bed, eating the last of the snacks." A hand on Avery's knee, he turns on the Rockies game that just started.

"Doug, hush!" He's barking at a pigeon that's sitting on the sleek aluminum balcony railing. The bird cocks its head and flies off.

My eyes keep flitting to Jason's hand. Such a casual touch; my sister barely even notices it. But I haven't been touched like that in months. I feel like the forgotten leftovers in the back of the fridge, moldy and uneaten.

"He had a bad day," I say to no one.

"More like a bad year," Avery mutters. "And what happened with Manuel? We saw him downstairs. He said something about Doug chasing him?"

Grimacing, I tell her the story. Avery's tiny facial features twist under her hip blond pixie. She's my older sister, but she's shorter and more petite. Also smarter and more successful.

She's an environmental engineer. I check in the clients of HHB and keep the attorneys' schedules straight. World-changing work it is not.

"What's going on with him these days?" Avery asks, watching Doug. "It's like he's gotten worse instead of better since . . . you know." She quit saying *since Tim left* because I couldn't stop flinching every time I heard the words. "There was that time at the dog park with your coworker. He looked like he wanted to rip his head off. Now this."

Max. A tingly feeling crawls up my spine every time I think of him. Max Rothschild is an associate attorney, hired a few months ago. We ran into each other at the dog park, and he sort of invited me to lunch, but when he brought it up again, I made an excuse. I'm not ready to date yet.

My laptop trills from the desk in my room. I jump to my feet. The Skype ringtone is my favorite sound in the world now.

Doug's too. He sprints into my room from the balcony, then hops on his back legs, trying to get into the desk chair. I lift him up and press the button to answer the video call.

Like every week, my heart lodges in my throat as I wait for it to connect. Doug's front paws are on the desk. He leans toward the screen. And . . . finally . . . we see him.

Tim's hair burns bright in the sun. His skin, tanned a deep bronze, is the perfect complement to his sapphire eyes. My naked left ring finger throbs painfully, something it's been doing randomly since Tim took off to Bali.

He's sitting at a table in the shade of a palm tree. A sliver of sand and ocean frame him. Soft music plays in the background, and a half-eaten plate of mango and papaya sits beside his hand. It's about five thirty here, so it's eight thirty in the morning, Tim's time.

"Hey, there's my boy!" he says.

Doug woofs and almost leaps onto the keyboard. A doggy smile stretches across his face, and Tim's grin broadens. "You miss me, buddy? I miss you!"

I pluck Doug gently off the desk, where he's leaving scratches, and put him in my lap. Tim's eyes flick from Doug to me. For a moment, I feel the full warmth of the Pacific sun on my face. As he looks back at Doug, the sun sets. I swallow hard.

"Hi," I say. "How are things going there?"

"Amazing. I met some investors this week who are really interested in my project. I'm meeting with one of them again in a few minutes, so I have to keep this short."

I blink. *Short? He just called!*

"That's great, Tim! Congratulations. I know how hard you've been networking there. So, if they decide to invest, will you be coming back soon?" I hate the pleading tone in my voice, but like the flinching with Avery, I can't seem to stop it.

Tim's excited expression drops off his face. "I don't know yet, Amelia, I mean, they haven't committed yet. And I haven't been here that long." His eyes shift to the side of the screen. He waves at someone.

"It's been over three months."

Irritation shoots across his gorgeous, familiar face. "We've talked about this. Global Ballers deserves a shot at success. To do that, I need money. Investors are here, so I'm here."

We had talked about it, many times. Tim left Colorado, and our relationship, to stay at a resort in Bali that brings entrepreneurs and wealthy people together in hopes of making an investing love match.

And Global Ballers, Tim's nonprofit, is a lovely idea. He wants to produce sturdy basketballs to distribute to poor kids around the world. As he says in his pitch, he's passionate about basketball and committed to bringing the joy of sports to children in need.

I just wish he could be passionate and committed somewhere closer than nine thousand miles away.

"I know, and I'm so proud of you. Doug and I just . . . we miss you."

Doug squirms toward him, his nails digging into my legs. I yelp, but Tim only frowns when Doug lets out a high-pitched whine.

"Is he okay? He sounds a little off."

"He had a rough day." *We both did*, I want to say.

"What happened?"

"He got into a bag of coffee while I was at work, and then he trapped Manuel in Avery and Jason's bedroom for half an hour until I got home and let him out."

Tim snorts before his eyebrows pinch together. "A whole bag of coffee?"

"Almost." I flush, feeling guilty again for leaving that tote on the ground. "Do you think he's okay? He's hyper tonight, but he's been a little down the last few weeks. He's not eating as well, and he's . . . grumpy."

Tim is the expert on all things Doug. He got him from a breeder about a year before we met and named him for his favorite pop artist, Lil' Dougie.

I might not have been there from the beginning, but I fell hard for both of them as soon as I met them. Tim and I were together for a year and lived together for the last six months until he got this grant to go to Bali.

I cringe away from thinking about the awful day I thought he'd propose, and instead he asked me to keep Doug while he was away. Too traumatic.

"He's due for a checkup soon," he says. "Maybe you should take him to that vet I emailed you the name of before I left."

"Okay." *Where did I put that email again?*

Doug shakes his head hard, like he disagrees. His sharp nails dig into my leg again as he tries to inch closer to the screen.

Tim looks to his side, nods, and smiles. That smoldering look that used to slide over his face when we first started dating slides over it now. I freeze. Who does he see? He'd said the investors he'd met were mostly old men, there in Bali with their trophy wives or mistresses.

"Who's that?" Jealousy turns my voice green. Okay, so we'd agreed to see other people before he left. Actually, *he'd* agreed we'd see other people, and I went along with it. But he hadn't told me he'd met anyone. *Would* he tell me?

"I have to go." Tim leans in a little and lowers his voice. "Let me know how it goes with that vet. Bye, Dougie. Love you, fella."

I wave Doug's front paw.

Love you, too, Amelia, Tim doesn't say, as my screen goes dark.

I carry Doug to my bed and lie down on my side. Looking dejected, he curls up next to me and licks my nose before settling in. His barrel chest expands and contracts as he breathes. Before long he's woofing in his sleep, his legs twitching as he chases dream squirrels.

I wish good dreams came so easy to me.

Chapter Three

On my break Monday afternoon, I search through old emails from Tim to find the name of the vet. I hoot through a mouthful of apple when I finally locate it, drawing looks from other people sunning themselves in the outdoor courtyard down the street from HHB. I smile at them, hoping I don't have red peel stuck in my teeth.

I look at the address. Aurora, Colorado? If I had a car, getting to the suburbs wouldn't be a big deal, but I use Lyft. Avery has a car . . . only I can't ask her to borrow it for Doug. She hates him right now for destroying her place.

Also, she thinks I'm a total pushover for taking Doug in when Tim left, but there's just something about that pug. I need him as much as he needs me.

Tim won't mind if I find a different vet somewhere downtown, will he? One I can walk Doug to?

I do a quick search on my phone. There are at least twenty-five. I scroll through them. Anyone specialize in mentally disturbed pugs?

Then I spot this listing: Love & Pets Mobile Animal Clinic, Travis Brewer, DVM. I click the link. A dark-haired guy, too small to see other than that he's wearing scrubs, stands with arms crossed in front of a turquoise-blue RV with a heart-shaped logo on the side. I smile. Cute.

Serving all parts of metro Denver, including downtown.

A mobile vet sounds great, nice and convenient. I call the number. An older woman answers, sounding out of breath. I make an appointment for Saturday morning, the next time Dr. Brewer will be downtown, she tells me. He parks at the dog park a few blocks from our apartment building to see patients. Perfect for me, and not bad advertising for them, I guess.

I walk back to work. Kenny sits at his place, down the long desk from my station by the front doors, typing studiously.

"Nice lunch?" he asks.

"If you call an apple and yogurt nice," I say. "Want to take your break?"

"Later. I need to finish these notes for Jim." He bends over the keyboard, the dark skin of his shaved head shining in the artificial lights over the desk. His shirt, vest, and slacks combo is so fabulous I want to take a picture and send it to one of those stock photo sites. He'd be a picture-perfect addition to a law office website.

As a legal assistant, Kenny's one step above me in the HHB food chain. He does much more important work than I do—like legal research and drafting documents for the partners—but he also has to answer the phone and greet clients for me when I'm out on my half-hour lunch break or when I use the restroom.

Not for much longer, though. He's starting law school in August. My heart droops. What will I do without him to talk at? I mean talk to?

I check my email and voice mail. Nothing. I can hear Jim, Cassie, Forty, and Max in the conference room, although not what they're talking about. It would be boring civil law stuff anyway. It's the Monday-afternoon staff meeting. I use my phone camera as a mirror while I refresh my lipstick, think about getting some tea but decide against it, and peek at Kenny.

"What are you doing tonight?" I ask.

He doesn't look up. "Studying."

"Still? Why? You're already in. What are you even learning?"

He rolls his eyes and stops typing. He hates when I interrupt him, but I can't help myself. "I got my first semester course list. I'm doing some pre-reading."

"Ruston must already hate law school." Kenny's partner is a florist, and from the sound of it he works just as hard. But still.

"He understands."

"How's your mom?" I ask.

"Still upset. She's taking it hard." His face softens.

I nod. She lost her pet chihuahua, Stinkers. I'd be devastated if something happened to Doug. "Is she thinking about getting a new dog?"

"Not yet. It's too soon." He glances at the door. "They're breaking up. Look busy."

I put my hand on my mouse and start clicking around in the scheduling program. Kenny can always tell when the partners are coming. I swear he either has supersonic hearing or he smells Max's sublime-scented aftershave lotion. Sure enough, the tall, frosted conference room door opens a moment later and the senior partners, plus Max, file out.

Jim Hand strolls through first, followed by his wife, Cassandra Hart, who talks at his back. Max holds the door open for Fortunatus Butz. With his stooped back, white hair, and too-short tie, Forty is a senior partner in more ways than one. He should be called Eighty.

"See you Wednesday?" Jim asks Forty, interrupting Cassie. She looks annoyed but stops talking.

Forty's hearing aid whines a little, and he grimaces. "Yes, I'll be back Monday."

Monday mornings are about the only time we see Forty. Which is too bad, because he's the only one of the senior partners I like.

"Right, Monday." Jim pats him on the back.

Forty winks at me as he leaves, and I wave. Jim swipes a hand over his disappearing hair and saunters to my desk.

"What's next, Amelia?" While his eyes meander down to my pink lemonade–colored blouse, Cassie turns her back on us to talk to Kenny and Max.

I sit up straight, eliminating any gaps Jim might peer down, and check his schedule. He can access it on his phone, computer, and tablet—not to mention the print copy I provide each of the partners every morning. But he loves for me to tell him every few hours anyway. I read him the rest of his appointments.

"Be sure everything's submitted for billing by the end of the day, will you?" He coughs and heads for the door, probably for a smoke break.

As soon as Jim takes off, it's Cassie's turn. I'm fascinated by the way her lips move . . . and nothing else. Despite being twice my age, her face is a wrinkle-, sunspot-, and expression-free zone. She must single-handedly keep some cosmetic surgeon in business. Not that I wouldn't do the same if I were that old.

"*Ameeelia*"—she draws out my name every time she says it—"I sent you an email with the itinerary for our trip to Vancouver next month. Be sure and schedule a stop in Seattle. We'll be meeting with clients there on the way."

I nod and struggle to smile. The stop in Seattle to see clients is crap. Before I started, Kenny scheduled Jim and Cassie's personal trips. He said they pretended to make it work-related so they could get us to make their travel plans for them. I wouldn't mind doing it if they'd just ask me nicely instead of lying about it.

"Yes, Cassie. I'll do it now."

She barely acknowledges I spoke, turning back to Max. I can feel his eyes on my face, but I don't look at him. Although he *is* incredibly pleasant to look at, with his perfectly cut and styled dark hair, light-blue denim eyes, tailored shirts and suits, and a chest like a topographic map just begging to be explored.

No, no, Amelia. Down girl.

And why am I lusting after Max? I love Tim. Period.

Cassie and Max speak for a minute about a case they're working on. Although I keep my head down, I see her glance at the door Jim disappeared out of. "Why don't I just show you? Come to my office."

It's an order, not a request. Max hesitates. I hope he's not staring at me. Cassie could care less if Jim looks down my shirt, but although she's old enough to be Max's mother, she gets jealous if he pays special attention to me. And when he does, she finds a way to take it out on me. Usually extra busy work on Friday afternoons.

Max is a hot potato, but best to leave that sizzling spud alone.

Saturday morning, I'm kneeling on the ground beside the door to our apartment, a squirming Doug in my hands, trying to get his collar on. He wants to go out—bad. I have to practically flatten him to snap it on and attach the leash. My sister watches, arms crossed and lips thin.

"Ready, Aves?" I ask breathlessly. "Thanks so much for coming with me."

I'm a total coward, but . . . I'm afraid to take Doug to the vet by myself. What if something's wrong with him? What will I do without him? What will I tell Tim?

Avery opens the door. Doug barks and lunges towards a poor guy who happens to be passing down the hall.

"Doug, no!" My hand scrapes against the door frame as he pulls me out. I yelp with pain.

The man scurries forward a few feet, out of the reach of Doug's snapping teeth, but Doug strains toward him anyway, growling. Avery and I stare at my dog, eyes wide.

"I'm glad you're taking him in," she says.

I nod and set my shoulders. He needs this.

Doug barks all the way down the hall, as if murderers and rapists, or at least depraved dog-bone thieves are about to pop out of every apartment door. Although I shush him, he only gets worse in the elevator.

We hustle the ten minutes to the dog park, Doug woofing and growling at passing men all the way. The park is a large, fenced in patch of dirt surrounded by four-story apartments. Dogs of all colors and sizes charge around inside while their owners hurl balls for them or gather in small groups to chat, ignoring the shenanigans.

Doug hops up and down against the chain link fence, wanting in, but I'm afraid to let him go off leash. There are at least ten men wandering around in there. I shudder, imagining what he might do to them if given the chance.

The Love & Pets–mobile isn't here yet, so Avery and I sit on a bench beside the half-full parking lot. Watching the other dogs run around sniffing butts makes Doug whine and pull on his leash.

An older woman with a messy salt-and-pepper bun sits on the bench beside us, knitting. Long, white dog fur covers her black t-shirt and baggy capris. She glances at Doug. "Looks like he wants to go in. Don't you, handsome boy?"

Avery gives the woman a look like she must be blind. I beam at the compliment. Doug can—and probably has been—called a lot of things, but with his overbite, wrinkles, and flat face, handsome isn't one of them.

"He does," I say. "But he's been having trouble getting along with people. We're actually waiting to meet a mobile vet here to talk about it."

"Oh, that's too bad. What's wrong, handsome?" she asks Doug with a pouting face. He glances at her. The tip of his tail wags, and he goes back to watching the other dogs.

"We aren't sure," I say. "Normally he's super sweet, but lately . . . he seems to have a problem with men."

The woman grunts in a tell-me-about-it kind of way. "So do I, so do I. What's his name?"

"Doug. My boyfriend—"

"*Ex*-boyfriend," Avery says, leaning around me to the woman.

"My ex-boyfriend named him after Lil' Dougie."

The woman's face lights up. She drops her knitting beside her, raises her hands to the sky, and belts out a spot-on imitation of the singer.

"Girl, I love you so bad, your love, it drives me mad . . ."

Avery and I laugh, but Doug goes stiff. He yanks the leash out of my hands, leaps into her lap, narrowly avoiding being stabbed by her knitting needles, and plants his paws on her chest. She screams. I dive toward them and scoop him up while Avery scrambles to pick up the yarn he sent flying.

"I'm so sorry," I say to the woman. He was only licking her face, but visions of what he could have done fly through my mind. "Bad Doug! Bad boy!"

Will she call animal control on us for having a clearly out-of-control dog? How do I explain that Tim used to sing that song every night to Doug, and now whenever he hears it, he loses it? I wait for her reaction, my arms tight around him.

The woman takes a tissue out of her battered purse, mops her face, and chuckles. "Whew! I haven't been kissed like that in years."

Avery and I burst out laughing, and I apologize again. After a minute, she goes back to knitting, and I sit down with Doug in my lap, fingers around his collar.

"What was that about?" Avery whispers to me, her eyes on Doug.

"I don't know. That's why we're here. Maybe it's just a phase?"

"Long phase." She doesn't say anything for a minute. "What will you do if he doesn't get over whatever this is? I mean, he's Tim's dog, not yours. Right?"

"He's both of ours." My voice is tight. Tim might have had Doug first, but he was mine as much as his now. "And I'll do whatever it takes to help him."

Doug quivers, his nose twitching as he sniffs the air. Avery shakes her head and mutters something under her breath.

Something *is* wrong with him, I know. And it definitely has to do with men. I can avoid the Lil' Dougie song, no problem. But guys are a different story. I scan the dog park and nearby apartments. At least half the people strolling around are male, of course. It's like a minefield of men out here. Chills of worry roll up and down my arms, settling in my shoulder blades.

Manuel could kick us out. Avery could decide she's had enough and boot Doug. I'm pretty sure she won't evict me with him, but if he goes, I go. Only . . . I can't afford an apartment on my salary. I moved to Denver after college because Avery was here, and because I didn't know where else to go. I definitely wasn't moving back in with Mom in Kansas City. Other than Tim's friends, I don't know many people in Denver. Maybe Kenny and Ruston will let me live in their basement? I imagine the look on Kenny's face if I asked him. Yeah. Doubtful.

A flash of bright blue catches my eye. The Love & Pets RV trundles down the street and bounces into the lot beside us. We stand and say good-bye to the woman.

"I hope he's all right," she says.

"Thanks, me too," I say.

She winks. "At least he's a good kisser."

Doug positively grins.

Chapter Four

The RV's engine turns off, and a tiny, frail woman slides out of the passenger seat.

She has almost waist-length gray hair, as thick as a tween girl's, and she wears long, dangly turquoise earrings and turquoise scrubs. Even her sneakers are the same shade of blue.

She rests with her hand on the passenger door for a moment, catching her breath, then she smiles at us. As soon as she speaks, I know it's the woman who made Doug's appointment when I called. Her voice is scratchy and thin.

"Hello, who is this?" She coughs a little at the end.

I smile tentatively. "Doug. We have an appointment with Dr. Brewer at ten."

The woman smiles, revealing a perfect set of white teeth. Definitely dentures. "Oh, yes, our new patient." She leans down to hold a hand out for Doug to sniff. I hold the leash tightly, just in case, but he only wags his tail after a good smelling. "I'm Jo, Dr. Brewer's vet tech. And you're Amelia?"

Before I can answer, the driver comes around the front of the RV. He's also wearing scrubs, although his are a less flashy navy blue. Travis Brewer, DVM, is young. Younger than I was expecting, anyway. Maybe twenty-six or twenty-seven, only a few years older than me. And definitely good looking, with dark hair in a short, slightly messy ponytail, intense dark eyes, and high cheekbones. He and the woman look alike. Are they family?

I'm so busy gawking at him, Avery has to elbow me in the ribs. "Yes, hi. I'm Amelia. And this is my sister Avery, and that's Doug." I point at my dog.

"I'm Dr. Brewer. Please call me Travis." He squats down a few feet away from Doug and extends his hand. "Hello, Doug."

Doug stares at him, ears erect, and . . . launches himself at the vet, growling and barking. He hits him squarely in the chest and knocks him backward onto the asphalt.

The leash almost jerks my shoulder out of the socket, but I hang on to the end and drag him backward and off Travis. Jo looks shocked; Avery covers her mouth in horror.

My gut twisting, I wind the leash several more times around my hand and stay far away as Doug barks furiously at the veterinarian. All the people in the dog park stare at us. Several curious dogs come running.

Travis dusts off his butt and stands. I don't see any blood at least.

"I am *so* sorry. I have no idea what's going on with him. But now you've seen why we're here."

Travis smiles, although worry lines sprout from the corners of his eyes as he looks at Doug. "No harm done. Come in, and we'll chat."

He helps Jo up into the back of the Love & Pets RV and then stands back so Avery, Doug, and I can climb in. Doug stops barking, but he's still growling, his hackles up and nose wrinkled. Travis stays well away. Once inside, I pull Doug to a small folding chair in the far back corner and put him firmly on my lap while hanging on to his collar.

The RV is as white and silver inside as it is blue outside, and as sparse as a medical-office. Behind the driver seat, three square cages are stacked and attached to the side of the RV. A long metal counter runs opposite the door with medical equipment sitting on either side of a small sink. Closed cabinets line the wall under and above the counter, and to my left at the back, a metal table is folded up against the side.

On the inside of the door, a poster advertises some kind of community fair in August for free vaccinations and low-cost veterinary services, sponsored by the Love & Pets Mobile Animal Clinic.

Jo reaches into a drawer for a clipboard. Avery stays up front by the seats. Keeping an evaluating eye on Doug, Travis pulls medical gloves from a box in a cabinet. Like the villain in an old Western, Doug's dark eyes never leave him.

"You completed your paperwork online, so I'll just get a few signatures first." Jo hands me the board, and after a quick scan, I sign the three pages.

I chew the inside of my mouth with worry. What's wrong with Doug? What if he bites the vet while he examines him? Can vets sue pet owners?

For now, Travis stays over by Amelia, while Jo pulls the examination table down. I can hear her breathing with the effort.

"That was a dramatic entrance," Travis says. "Some of my patients like those." His smile is warm, warm enough that I relax a little. "So tell me what's been going on with Doug?"

Tears threaten to spill again, so I take a long breath. "What he did to you . . . that's basically why we're here. A few months ago, Doug was a sweet dog. He still is, sometimes." I glance at Avery, who raises an eyebrow. "With women at least. But then he does things like *that*." I point to the door. "I made the appointment after he trapped our building manager, Manuel, in a bedroom when he came in to do some work. I had to rescue him."

Travis and Jo chuckle, and I realize it does sound funny. Doug is maybe twenty pounds, and Manuel is tattooed and at least six feet tall. But my smile fades.

"I'm really worried about him."

The vet's face grows serious. "I understand. Small dogs can cause just as much damage as big dogs if given the chance." He steps closer, and I feel Doug tense. His body trembles.

"He's had his vaccinations, like rabies, right?" When Travis's black eyes flick to mine, a strange moth gets loose in my chest, fluttering around.

"Yes, at least, that's what I was told. He actually belongs to my boyfriend."

Did I imagine it, or did Travis' smile fade a touch?

Avery's jaw clenches noticeably. "Her *ex*-boyfriend."

The vet glances at her and then his eyes find Doug again. He moves a little closer, but Doug isn't relaxing.

Folding his arms, which I can't help notice are long, tan, and lean, Travis settles back against the counter. "How has he been acting, other than more aggressive?"

I consider. "He's been kind of quiet at home. Like he's sad, maybe. Not as excited for walks or trips to the dog park."

"Is he eating okay? Urinating and defecating normally? Any vomiting?"

I shake my head.

"No problems peeing, either," Avery says sarcastically.

I wilt. "I've had him for three months. I'm trying to take good care of him, but I don't think I'm doing a good job. He seems . . . unhappy."

"Has anything else been different in his environment recently?"

I pet Doug, and he rests against my chest a little. "Tim, my . . . ex-boyfriend has been out of the country. He video calls every week, but I think Doug really misses him. But, is that possible for dogs to miss people like that? Enough to make themselves miserable?"

Travis nods. "Dogs are very social creatures. Pack animals. They miss members of the pack when they're away, and especially pack leaders."

"That's Tim, all right," Avery says.

"When is he coming back?" he asks me.

I shrug. *I wish I knew.* "He was only supposed to be gone for six months, but now he's saying he may stay in Bali longer."

Travis's thick eyebrows raise. "Bali? Lucky guy."

He eyes me as he says this, and I feel my face flush.

"I just wish I knew what I could do for Doug to make him feel better being with me. More . . . secure. And, I'm really worried he's going to hurt someone."

"I have some ideas. But first I'd like to try to do a physical examination." He sidles closer again, standing next to Jo and the table. Doug stands up on my knees. I keep a firm hold on him.

"Are you sure?" I ask as Jo reaches inside a glass jar for a dog treat.

"If it's okay, we'll muzzle him during the exam to be on the safe side."

I agree. He'll hate it, but anything to keep him from biting.

"Put him up on the table, and I'll get the muzzle on quick as a wink," Jo says. Travis moves away again, and I set Doug down. His feet slip and toenails claw the metal as he tries to get off. Jo's thin fingers move quickly to slide the muzzle on his snout and secure it —not an easy task on a flat-faced pug. Doug's eyes roll up to me and he whines, but thankfully he doesn't growl or snap at Jo.

As Travis watches, Avery checks him out. I can't blame her. He is totally worth eyeballing. I try not to stare, I really do, at how his arm muscles contract when he reaches for Doug. Jo takes gentle hold of Doug, and I step back, staying where he can see me.

Doug shakes and growls softly as Travis examines his eyes, inside his ears, and his nose and mouth, as much as he can. He runs his hands over his sides, chest, belly, and neck with expert movements.

Jo pulls a scale out of a lower cabinet and sets it on the table. Travis lifts Doug on to it.

"Twenty-one pounds," Travis says. "That's a good weight for him. He's on the smallish side for a male pug, really. How much exercise is he getting?"

I wrinkle my nose. "We live in an apartment, so I walk him three times a day. But he might not be getting out as much as he used to." Neither was I.

"I don't see anything obviously wrong with him, but I'd like to get a temperature, take some blood, and run a blood-chemistry panel."

He twists to look at Avery, then back at me. "Anyone get sick at the sight of blood? If so, you might want to step outside."

We shake our heads. Jo holds Doug as Travis lifts Doug's tail and inserts a thermometer, keeping it there for a few seconds. Doug stiffens and growls, but really, who wouldn't? Then Travis swabs the skin of Doug's front right leg with alcohol, inserts a needle, and draws two vials of dark red blood. After, Travis takes off his gloves and washes his hands at the sink while Jo removes the muzzle.

"I'll send this off to the lab and be in touch as soon as the results come back. Can I call you at—" He reads my number from the clipboard.

Yes, please do. I shush my traitorous inner voice. "That's me."

"Great. Let's see what we find and touch base in a few days. Assuming Doug's blood chemistry comes back okay, then I'll have some ideas about behavioral interventions for him. He might benefit from training and maybe more socialization with other dogs."

Jo smiles and offers Doug to me. As I take him, he squirms around in my arms to keep his eye on Travis. I sigh.

Travis touches my elbow. "Try not to worry, Amelia. I'll do everything I can to help Doug."

Something about the quiet, calm confidence in his words warms my body, as if he'd said he'd do everything he could to help *me*.

"Given his reactions to men," Jo says, her voice kind, "you might want to take this. Put it on him when he's around people, and it'll give you some peace of mind."

She holds out the muzzle. It's only a piece of sturdy cloth with a snap that secures it behind the neck, but I hesitate to take it. I hate thinking about him having to wear it. How did we get here? Doug isn't *dangerous*.

I think of Manuel, then Travis. Even the singing lady. Okay, maybe he is.

"It's for his protection as much as other people's," Travis says. "He can get in big trouble if he bites."

I take it. "I understand. Thank you."

"You're walking home?" Jo asks. "Let me show you how to slip it on easy." She gives me a quick lesson and leaves it on Doug's head. I put him down, and he scratches at the thing. Poor guy looks like Hannibal Lector.

Avery and I thank them both. Jo opens the door for us. Doug scrambles out, jerking me off balance. I stumble and feel a hand under my arm. Travis. His palm is warm against my skin.

"Careful," he says. "The stairs are steep."

My face hot again, I thank him. Our eyes lock, and he nods. Then he looks past me. "Justin. Good to see you. Come on in."

A young guy with no hair on his head but wearing a full red beard and combat boots carries something reptilian in a cat carrier past us and into the RV.

The moment the door closes, Avery turns to me. "Holy hot vet, Mel. Travis is *gorgeous*."

I nod. He is, but I'm too worried about Doug to give his vet a lot of thought. Doug shakes his head hard and scratches the muzzle one more time. Giving up, he lifts his leg beside a bush.

Avery takes my arm as we walk. "Amelia, seriously though. Why do you still call Tim your boyfriend?"

"I don't know. I guess . . . I hope he will be again when he gets home." I watch Doug trotting ahead of us. He looks a little downcast. "Aves, right or wrong, I still love Tim. And even with all his faults, I love Doug. I have to find a way to help him."

"I wasn't so sure when I saw that blue RV pull up, but Travis and Jo seem great. Maybe they can help him be a good dog again," Avery says.

I hope so, but when it comes to Doug that seems a lot easier said than done.

Chapter Five

I feed Doug in my room that evening, slipping him pieces of dog food one by one. His snout is velvet against my palm as he nibbles them. When he's behaving, he's the most adorable thing I've ever seen.

An exasperated noise comes from the open door behind me. Avery. "Okay Mel, I know you love Doug, but you spend too much time with him. So I have a new plan. Travis will figure out how to re-socialize Doug, and I'm going to re-socialize you. You're coming out with Jason and me tonight."

I groan. "No Aves. I'm not up to it." I cough. "My throat is scratchy. I could have a summer cold coming on."

She plops down on my bed. Her hair is wrapped in a towel, and she's wearing a robe. She holds her gleaming coral-colored finger-nails out—fresh manicure.

"All right, get ready; I'm about to bring the sister hammer down. It's time to stop moping about Tim and meet someone new. Seriously. You've gotta move on, Mel."

Finished with his meal, Doug rolls on his back beside me so I can rub his belly. He wiggles back and forth, loving it.

Avery shakes her head. "I'm not kidding. You're going out with us."

"I'm tired, Aves, I just want to stay in and read or watch a movie or something."

"No. You're going to wear that royal-blue mini dress I gave you, put on some makeup and heels, and shake your bod. The guys will pant after you, and you'll remember why Tim fell hard for you in the first place."

I tuck my pajama-covered knees under my chin and stare at Doug. "He did fall for me once, didn't he? I'm not imagining that?"

She sits beside me and pulls my head against her shoulder, keeping her fingernails clear of my hair. "Of *course* he did. Why wouldn't he? You're beautiful, kind, and you can wrangle lawyers with the best of them. Plus, you're my sister. Which gives you, like, thirty bonus points."

I snort.

"Mel, getting your heart broken sucks. It does. And it takes a while to get over. But you can't hide from the world forever. Life is more than work, sleep, and a pug." She scratches Doug's head, and he licks her hand.

Is it? With a shaky breath, I nod.

"Maybe if you relax and have fun, Doug will, too."

My hand stops moving in circles on his chest. Could he be taking his cue from me? "I hadn't thought of that."

"So, you'll come?"

I kiss her cheek and lean over to kiss the back of Doug's neck. "Okay. I'll go."

"You're the best sister, ever. Have I told you that?"

I'm leaning into Avery. The music in the club is pumping, so I have to scream at her to be heard. Did I spit on her a little? *Oops.*

"You told me, Mel." Her voice sounds funny—flat.

"About ten times," Jason says beside her. I try to focus on him, his olive skin and dark hair, but his two pesky faces won't come together. At least he's smiling.

When I hold my glass to my lips to take a drink, liquid avalanches over the rim and down my blue dress, the one Avery told me to wear. Fascinated, I watch the wet spot spread and grow across my chest. Like my heart burst and leaked from the inside out. Ewww.

"Whoops." My voice sounds funny, too. I giggle.

Jason hands me a napkin, and I blot at the stain.

"I love you, Jason," I say. "You know that, right? You should marry my sister. Then you could be my brother!"

"Amelia!" Avery hisses.

I lean closer. "What? He should. You're such a catch, Aves. She's really smart, Jason. An environmental engineer." I take a few tries to get *environmental engineer* out right.

Avery's face swims between mine and his. "He's an engineer, too. We met at my last job, remember?"

I don't. But I can't remember much right now. Except the four vodka tonics I'd sucked down. Now *those*, I remember. A little voice in the back of my head warns me I haven't seen the last of them, but I ignore her.

A person walks by our table, hesitates, then stops. The alcohol-veiled version of the guy is a swathe of dark hair on a nice body. Blue eyes and fair skin. Some sort of clothing.

"Amelia?" he says.

I blink and peer at him, but he won't stay still so I can recognize him.

"Mel." Avery loud-whispers in my ear. "It's that guy from the dog park a few months ago. He's talking to you."

"The dog park?" My eyes keep sinking to his chin. He has a nice chin. Clean shaven. Nothing like a dog's whiskery chin.

"It's Max." He looks like something about me is funny.

"Max! Right! Hi!" I say.

A warning bell rings in my head. Why? I try to stand to shake his hand, or maybe hug him. I'll bet he's wearing that aftershave I love. I lean toward him to find out and stumble back into my seat. That's okay. There's two ways to skin that cat.

"What does that even mean?" I ask Avery.

"What?" she asks.

"Nothing. Um, want to sit?" I ask Max, then shove down the bench into Avery, making room.

He slides in the booth beside me and looks at me like he expects something. What could it be? Finally, he leans around me and holds out his hand to Avery. He has strong hands. Strong, good for holding and carrying things. Like, me, maybe. Hmm.

"Hi, I'm Max. We met at the dog park."

My sister elbows me—on purpose, I think—while reaching to shake his hand.

"Ow." I rub my upper arm and give her a hurt look, but she ignores me and smiles at Max.

"I remember. I'm Avery, Amelia's sister."

Jason introduces himself to Max. Their voices get all low and firm like it's a growling competition. I snort.

"You work with Mel, right?" Avery asks. Her expression looks too bright. Kind of fixed, like she looks when she's embarrassed. Why is she embarrassed? She's acting totally fine.

"I'm a new associate at HHB."

"No Heart, All Hands, and Very Little Butz." I giggle again.

Avery rolls her eyes, and Max squints like he doesn't understand my joke.

"Get it? Jim: all hands, or he would be if I let him. Cassie: no heart. And poor Forty is so skinny. Kenny and I made it up." I snort, proud of my wit. Really I made it up, Kenny just listened and typed, like he always does.

Max smiles. Sexy. Very sexy. He lowers his voice so only I can hear. "Clever. Do you have a name for me, too?"

My pointer finger waggles back and forth. "Yes, but I can't tell you."

"C'mon. I'd like to know." His breath smells like whiskey. And he *is* wearing my favorite aftershave. I breathe deep, sniffing him like Doug sniffs the taco food truck that parks on our block sometimes.

"Nope. Can't," I say.

I realize my shoulder, arm, and the side of my boob are pushing against his firm arm. I melt into him. I haven't leaned against a man in *so* long. It feels good. *He* feels good. What would the rest of him feel like?

"Do you want to dance, Max?" I ask.

"Mel—" Avery says, "are you sure?"

Max takes my hand. "It's okay. I've got her."

I swivel my head between them. Do I need to be gotten?

He holds my hand to lead me to the dance floor. My ankle turns in my too-high heels, and he grabs my waist to keep me from falling.

"You okay?" he asks.

"I've had too many drinks, Max. Three too many. I'm a soft weight. A weight light. A—"

"A lightweight?"

I try to touch his nose to show him he got it, but miss and poke him in the cheek. "Lightweight. That's it. That's me. I don't usually drink," I hiccup, "this much."

"Dancing," he takes me in his arms, "is the cure to drinking too much. Work it out."

Thankfully the song is slow. If it had been fast, I was reasonably sure I'd end up on the sticky dance floor.

"I thought you were a lawyer, not a doctor."

He laughs, and I press closer. The warmth of him feels nice. *Soooo* nice. I've definitely missed this.

"How do you like working at HHB?" he asks.

"Not much. It's boring. But I love Kenny. Only he's leaving to be one of you." I pat him on the chest. "A big-shot attorney." I peer up at him. "Do you like being a big-shot attorney?"

"Sure."

"What do you like about it?"

"Law's an interesting field." He spins me around. The giant vodka martini inside me is shaken *and* stirred. My stomach lurches, and I swallow hard.

"Interesting how?" I really want to know. I spend all my time scheduling appointments for Jim, Cassie, and now Max, calling and reminding clients when to be there, and creating invoices and stuff. What I don't really know is *why* I'm doing it. What's the point?

He thinks about it. "I like helping people solve problems. It's a prestigious career. And—"

His watch winks in the lights of the dance floor. Looks expensive. I hold up that hand. "And it pays well."

He chuckles. "That doesn't hurt."

I stand on my tiptoes so my face is a few inches from his. His *lips* are a few inches from my lips. I stare at them. "I'll bet you like the power. Do you like having power over other people, Max?"

He raises an eyebrow. "Are you sure you aren't a psychologist in your spare time?"

"No. But I saw one once when my mom thought I was depressed in high school."

"Were you?"

"No, I was sad after breaking up with my boyfriend. She didn't think that was a good enough reason to be sad, so she paid someone hundreds of dollars to find another reason."

His hand sweeps down my back, just shy of my butt, and he dips me slightly. "Didn't you break up with another guy recently?"

Pain shoots through my head, and I stand up straight, almost bumping my forehead into his. I sway with the sudden movement, but he holds me up easily.

"Yes. Only he broke up with me."

Max slides his fingers across my cheek, down my neck, and into my hair. "I'd pay a psychologist to see *him* and find out why. If he broke up with you, he must have problems."

A tingling that has nothing to do with vodka runs through my body. I lay my head on his shoulder and wrap myself around him. He rubs circles into my low back, the way I do with Doug sometimes.

I'm sweating. Like, trickles of it around my hairline and down my spine. My face and chest prickle. *Pull yourself together, Amelia. Max is hot, but c'mon.*

When my stomach clenches and spit pools in my mouth, I realize the sweat has nothing to do with Max . . . and everything to do with the vodka.

I push away from him. "I need to go to the restroom."

Max follows, I think, as I stagger back to our table. Acid burns my throat, and I swallow repeatedly. *No no no no.* Not in front of Max.

"Avery!" I wail.

With one glance at me, my sister jumps up.

"I'm going to be sick." I loud whisper.

"It's okay, Melly. C'mon. Let's hurry."

Max stands nearby. I can't look at him; I'm too humiliated.

"I'm sorry—she'll talk to you later, okay?" Avery says to him.

"Feel better, Amelia," he says.

I wave back at him, but my focus narrows until all I can see is a path through the crowd to the toilet that must be back there somewhere.

At least if I puke on someone on the way, and they sue, I know who to call.

Chapter Six

The next morning I lie in bed in sick, sweaty, head-pounding misery.

I need to apologize to Avery, Jason, and Max from work. I feel sure I do, but I'm not positive exactly *why*.

Doug whines from his crate. He usually sleeps with me, but Avery must have stuck him in there, afraid I wouldn't get up and he'd pee. I should take him out.

I try to sit, and the room whirls around me like I'm hanging on one of those spinning things at the playground. Why did I have all those drinks again? I close my eyes and drift off. I can't face the day.

Sometime after that, Avery bursts into my room. She throws open my curtains and perches on the end of my bed. Doug bounds in the room after her, launches himself onto my bed, and licks my face. The smell of his breath is sickening.

"Morning Mel-Belle. How do you feel?" Is she screaming on purpose?

My tongue sticks to the roof of my mouth. "Like King Kong pogo-sticked on my head last night."

"Four vodka tonics will do that to you." She hands me a small family of ibuprofen and a glass of water.

I try to sit up again, but the great ape isn't finished with me yet. Groaning, I toss the pills in my mouth, sip some water, and slide back down.

I squint at my phone on the bedside table. It's noon. I struggle up a third time. "I have to . . . take Doug out."

"Jay and I took him a few hours ago. Fed him, too."

"You did?"

She shrugs. "He was whining." She picks up my phone. "So that guy, Max?"

I cover my eyes. "Oh no. What. What did I do? Did I kiss him? What?" I gasp. "He didn't see me get sick, did he?"

"No, although it was close. You only made it to the fake plant in the bathroom hallway."

I groan, remembering now. It was a palm tree.

"Actually, he left you this." She hands me my phone. Someone had typed in *Max* and a number.

"He gave me his number?" I blink at it. "*Why?*"

"No idea." Avery says seriously. "He must be the care-taking type. Or desperate. But he doesn't look like he should be."

My brain aches trying to remember what Max and I talked about. Something about why he was a lawyer. And that I'd seen a psychologist. And Tim. I groan.

"Just delete the contact," I say. "After last night, I'm quitting HHB so I'll never have to see him again." Doug wiggles under one hand, wanting me to scratch him. Distractedly, I do.

"Too late. I already texted him from you," Avery says.

"What?" I shoot up, and my head throbs angrily. "What did you say?"

"I invited him to dinner. A dinner that you're going to help me make."

I clutch my neck. "Please tell me you're kidding."

"Sorry, but no. Max seems like a nice guy. He has a dog, so he must like them. He gave you his number even after he saw you at your—and believe me, I mean this—your worst. And mainly because it's time for you to get over Tim."

"But *dinner*? That's like . . . You invited him on a . . ." I almost pant, trying to keep the panic at bay.

"Yeah. I invited him on a date with you," she says. "Time to rejoin life, Amelia. It's nice out here. You'll like it."

Chapter Seven

That evening, barely an hour after the headache and nausea finally fade away, I sit on the couch in a sensible pair of jeans, flats, and a summer-weight white sweater, drinking water.

Avery fixed my hair in a loose braid. Every time I tried to do it myself, my hands shook too bad to get it right. She says I look pretty, but I don't feel human enough to tell for myself.

I managed to take Doug out and clean up his poop—from the middle of the sidewalk, of course—without dry heaving. Now, he lies on his side on the balcony in a patch of sunlight, asleep. At least, until the doorbell rings. When it does, he races to the door, barking like the entire North Korean army must be on the other side.

Avery yells from the kitchen for me to get it, but I'm frozen with fear. I haven't dated in almost a year and a half. Max is my coworker. Yes, he's hot as a habanero. But I still love Tim.

I'm not ready for this.

Jason pops his head out of the kitchen. After a questioning glance at me, he heads for the door. "I got it."

I pick up Doug and hold him. Then I don't have to do anything I might regret, like hug Max or kiss him on the cheek. He would probably smell like the aftershave. Or like soap or laundry detergent. Anyway, he'd smell like a *man*.

Doug is the only man I've smelled up close in so long, and he smells like Fritos.

"Hey, Max. Good to see you again, man." Jason shakes his hand and lets him in.

Oh, good golly.

Max might have looked good last night. I wasn't in any condition to remember. But tonight . . .

His dark hair is wavy, still damp from the shower. He made an effort, too, wearing nice jeans and a tailored white collared shirt with no wrinkles. He smiles at me, showing his dimples and perfect white teeth.

This is not fair. No man should make you tremble just looking at him. I cradle Doug and wave a little. Doug growls, his ears at attention.

"Hi again," Avery says from behind me. "Thanks for coming."

"Of course." Max winks at me. "Had to be sure Mel was still alive."

"I'll be honest. It was touch and go there for a while." Avery says. They all laugh and look at me.

I wince. "Max . . . I'm . . . so sorry about last night."

I only manage to stare at his feet, clad in loafers. He has an actual sense of style, I realize, like a man instead of an overgrown boy. When Tim wasn't dressed for work, he wore T-shirts and basketball shorts.

As if he heard me think of Tim, Doug barks at Max.

Max's eyes crinkle. "Hey, boy. Doug, right?"

"That's right." I'm surprised, and weirdly touched, that he remembers.

Although Doug sounds ready to tear Max's hand off, Max reaches to pet him. Sure enough, Doug snaps, barely missing Max's thumb. Max and I both jump back.

"Doug! No, no! Bad dog." I need something else to say. All that bad dog stuff definitely isn't working with Doug.

Avery throws me an exasperated look. "Maybe he should go in his crate?"

"Good idea." I hurry to my room, pop him in, and close my door on his pathetic whining.

"What'll you have to drink?" Jason asks Max. "Beer, wine, or . . . what do you say, Mel?" He smirks. "I think we have a little hair of the dog that bit you."

I shake my head carefully, and with as much dignity as I can locate. "I'll stick with water, thank you."

I'd never touch alcohol again. At least not for a few days.

Max asks for a beer. I fetch it, then put the bread loaf in the oven. The salad is already prepped. Avery and Jason made pork chops. I can almost hear Doug salivating from here.

I was a vegetarian when I was with Tim, because he was, but I'd been eating a little meat again the last month. Avery said I needed the energy.

"How are you feeling?" Max asks when I come out.

"*Mostly* myself." I smile.

"Rough night, huh?"

"Yeah, it was bad. Except for seeing you there." My eyes widen with shock. Did I just say that out loud?

He grins and settles onto the couch, and I sit next to him while Avery and Jason finish up in the kitchen. He puts a casual arm behind me.

"Anyway," I say quickly. "How was your . . . weekend?" I can't think of anything else to ask. I don't know much about Max, I realize. And I can't focus. Doug's alternating between barking and whimpering from his crate.

"Good. I did some climbing with friends."

"You climb?" That explains his rock-hard bod.

"I picked it up during law school. I try to go every weekend, and I climb at the gym for exercise during the week."

I eye Avery, who's by the table. A lot of people in Colorado are married to their sport. Jason, for example, loves mountain biking. Avery doesn't, but she goes with him so she can spend time with him. She figures if she can't beat it, she'll join it, even if it means she doesn't get to do the things *she* loves as much.

I ask which gym he goes to, but I don't hear his answer. Doug is making noises I've never heard him make, a series of short, sharp barks strung together with low howls that sound like screams. Did I shut his paw in the crate when I closed the gate or something?

"Is he okay?" Max asks. I think he can tell I'm not listening.

"I don't know. Maybe I should check on him." I stand.

Avery pauses while setting the table. "He's *fine*, Amelia. Come sit. Dinner's ready."

As we pass the food around, I struggle to find something to talk about. Now that Max is here, sitting at our table, I feel weird. Like the beautiful, mysterious abstract painting in Cassie's office, Max is something to stare at and wonder about, not talk to.

And . . . he belongs at work, not in our dining room.

"So, are you from Colorado?" Avery finally asks. I shoot her a grateful look.

"No, Michigan. I came out for law school after skiing at Vail with some friends in high school. How about you?" He looks at me.

"We're from Kansas City. I moved to Denver after college because Avery was working here."

"KC. Nice. I'm a big Chiefs fan."

I smile politely, but I hate football. I was thrilled Tim loved another sport instead.

"Chiefs, huh?" Jason says. "No love for the Lions?"

Max makes a face. "What's to love?"

I munch on salad while they debate who will have good teams this year, and who might be traded with whom in the draft. Who cares, is what I *want* to say. But at least it's not awkward silence. When Jason starts talking about his short-lived career as a professional mountain biker, I tune them out.

Doug's constant whines are so sad. I wish I could spring him. If Max wasn't here, I could.

Avery kicks me in the shin, and I jolt. She tilts her head at Max and bugs her eyes. *Talk to him*, she's saying. Or at least listen. I shake my head a little, and she tips her head toward the kitchen. I'm about to get a lecture; I stand with a sigh.

Max holds up his empty beer bottle as I pass. "Can I grab another?"

I take it with a forced smile. "Sure."

She pulls me into the pantry, which isn't easy to do, and puts her mouth near my ear. "Amelia, I know I asked Max to come over and everything, but you're not even trying."

"I'm not up for this. I have a headache."

"That's not it, and you know it."

"I don't like him."

"How do you know? You've barely said two sentences together to him."

"He's . . . too good looking. And I don't like football. Or climbing. Remember that time I tried climbing club in high school? I almost *died* when Jamie Wilson let go of the belay."

She rolls her eyes. "Don't be dramatic. You fell on a mat. Your butt was bruised at most."

I wave Max's empty bottle around before letting it fall in the recycling bin behind me. "He didn't even say please when he asked for another beer."

"Ugh. Here." She ducks into the fridge, grabs one, and hands it to me. "Make. An. Effort."

I roll the beer in my hands. "Doug doesn't like him. How can I date someone Doug doesn't like?"

Amelia sticks her palm in my face, then points in the dining room. "I can't even. Go."

Guilt sloshes through me. I know she's right. What kind of hostess am I? Max is a nice enough guy. I need to get over myself and at least participate in the conversation. I straighten my back, smile, and gear up to be the bubbly, chatty Amelia that's in here somewhere, sometimes.

But as the food on our plates disappear, Avery tosses the real bomb at me, the one she's been carrying all night.

"Oh, crap. What time is it?" She looks at Jason.

"Sixish?"

"We're supposed to meet Chloe and Yolan at Jazz in the Park tonight, remember?"

He nods, his expression serene. Whatever this evil plan is, he knew about it beforehand.

She jumps up. "I'm so sorry you guys, but we have to go. You don't mind cleaning up, do you, Amelia?"

She doesn't wait for an answer, heading instead down the hall to her room. I excuse myself to follow her.

I duck behind her door. "What are you *doing*?"

She grabs a brush and runs it through her thick hair. "Forced reintegration. You need to spend a little alone time with a man who doesn't have four legs and a squashy face." She stops brushing and turns to me. "You feel safe with Max, right? I mean you don't get creeper vibes from him, do you?"

"No, but—"

"And it's not like he'll stay long. We all have to work tomorrow."

"Yes, but—"

"Then it's settled." She puts her hands on my arms. "Relax, Mel. Have fun. You're twenty-five, not seventy-five. Live a little." She kisses my cheek. "I'm doing this for your own good, because I love you. You know that, right?"

I nod, but I can't help thinking: if love is inviting over a guy I completely humiliated myself in front of without telling me and leaving me alone with him, then what did hate look like?

After hurried good-byes with Max, Avery and Jason take off. Leaving me alone with him. Which obviously doesn't seem as weird to him as it does to me.

Men and women do have dinner, clean dishes, and watch TV or whatever together, Amelia. I knew that, but I hadn't done it myself in months. I'm totally rusty.

After we get the table cleared and dishes into the dishwasher, I'm not sure what to do. I almost suggest we go down to the bar at the corner for a drink. That seems less . . . intimate. But before I decide, Max settles on the couch and turns the TV on like he owns the place.

What if he *is* a creeper or a rapist? My scalp gets hot and sweat pools in my armpits. I can't do this. I can't breathe. . . . Need . . . fresh . . . air.

"I need to take Doug out," I blurt.

"Yeah, a walk sounds good." He stands. "And I've never properly met the little guy."

I glance at him. He seems genuinely interested in meeting Doug, despite Doug's behavior, and at least we won't be snuggled up on the couch. "Okay. I'll get him."

I go into my room, grab Doug's leash and muzzle, and kneel down by the crate. He's curled up, facing away from the metal gate, toward the back.

"Doug? Sweetie? Want to go for a walk?" Those words usually bring on hysterics of happiness, but not today. He doesn't move. "Doug?" I shake the leash. Nothing. So I open the gate.

And that was my fatal mistake. In one smooth move, he leaps to his feet and charges out of the crate, barking angrily.

I fall backward against the side of my bed. "Doug, no! Stop!"

He races out of my room and turns the corner toward the living room—and Max—who lets out a shriek I've never heard from a man before. I run in.

Doug's teeth are firmly embedded in Max's arm. Max howls and tries to shake him off. No dice. Doug hangs on, his body slinging back and forth.

"Get him off me!" Max shouts.

I rush to them, hands flailing. I can't pull Doug off or he might take a chunk of Max's arm with him. It's a horror show of pug proportions.

An idea hits, something I saw on Animal Planet. I grab a blanket off the couch and bring it up and around Doug's body and head. Sure enough, as soon as his eyes are covered, he lets go, and I wrestle him to the ground, bringing the ends of the blanket together to trap him. He fights to get out, but I don't let go.

My eyes find Max's. Holding his arm, he looks like he's considering kicking Doug, or maybe me, so I move us farther away.

Both hands clutching the demon-possessed blanket, I whisper, "Max, meet Doug."

Chapter Eight

Max won't look at me the next day at work, and when I try to apologize again, won't speak to me. The bite isn't obvious under his shirtsleeve, but he keeps that arm close and winces as he reaches for his coffee cup during our staff meeting.

I feel terrible. I did what I could to help, but Max wasn't having it. After I stuffed Doug back in his crate, I tried to tend the bite. I offered to wash and bandage it or to take Max to the emergency room. He would only take a towel to wrap his arm in, and firm jaw set and beautiful blue eyes furious, he left.

Then, this evening, while surfing the internet with Doug on my bed, I get an email.

Dear Ms. Rhodes,

Please find a bill attached for the medical treatment and rabies vaccination I required after the vicious attack by your dog. I expect to receive payment in full within the week.

You may also receive a summons to court regarding your ownership of a dangerous dog. According to Colorado statute § 18-9-204.5, any owner whose dog inflicts bodily injury upon any person commits a class 3 misdemeanor, and the dog in question can be destroyed.

I will consider whether to take legal action in the matter and inform
you at my earliest convenience.
Sincerely,
Maxwell Rothschild, Esq.

Clutching my phone, I rush out of my room to find Avery. Doug
charges after me, yipping. Music drifts in from the balcony. My
sister's painting her toenails a vivid shade of purple. Hand shaking,
I hold out my phone to show her Max's email.

She sucks in a breath. "This is bad."

"I know. Do you really think he'd call animal control on Doug?
What if he . . . ? What if Doug . . . ?"

I shiver and pick Doug up to cradle him. I know he did an
awful thing in biting Max like that, but he needs help, not
destruction.

What would I do without him? What would I tell Tim?

"Don't think about that." Avery rubs my back. "What a jerk.
Doug shouldn't have attacked him, but still, you guys are cowork-
ers. Does he need to lawyer up over it? I'm sorry I invited him
over. And *really* sorry I gave him two of those craft beers Jason was
saving."

I sit down beside her, looking out at the faceless apartment
building across the street as Doug jumps in my lap. He looks so sad
and apologetic now.

This isn't what I wanted. None of it.

I didn't want Tim to leave. I didn't want to have dinner with
Max. I didn't want him to be hurt. And now, I might lose the one
thing that I *do* want—Doug.

"I'm calling Tim." Saying the words, I instantly feel better.

Avery's lips pucker like she's sucking a lemon drop. "It's the
middle of the night there, isn't it?"

"Yes, but this is an emergency. He said that was okay."

"Big of him," she mutters.

"You want to call Daddy?" I ask Doug.

I swear if a pug's face can light up, his does. He lets out one sharp, excited bark.

In my room, I plop him on the bed, where he playfully growls at my pillows and grabs and shakes a dirty sock I left there. I fire up Skype. It rings long enough that I don't think Tim's going to answer, until he does.

He's sitting in front of his laptop in the mostly-dark—bare chested, hair wild, and eyes slitted. I can just make out his rumpled bed behind him. An ache settles in my chest.

"Hello?" He mumbles in a sleep-sexy voice that makes my toes curl, but it's nothing to Doug's reaction. He leaps into my lap, barking, whining, and wiggling. I have to put him in a gentle head-lock to keep him from scrambling onto my laptop.

"Hey, Dougie. How are you?" Tim says, sounding more awake now. Doug struggles to get to him. "You look okay, at least."

What did that mean? Did I look bad?

"What's up, Amelia? It's pretty late here. Or early. I'm not sure."

I smooth my hair, self-conscious now along with panicked. "Doug attacked someone yesterday. He bit his arm pretty bad, and now the guy is threatening to take me to court over it and . . . and to maybe to report Doug to animal control. He called him a dangerous dog. Tim—he could be euthanized."

Tim rubs his face. "Start from the beginning, Amelia. What happened exactly?"

When I tell him the whole story, he looks as worried as I feel.

"Who's this Max guy?"

I hold Doug closer and shrug. "A guy from work. Avery, Jason, and I saw him at a bar this weekend and she invited him to dinner."

Tim's eyes open wider, and he blinks. "What does he do?"

"He's an associate. Avery invited him."

Why am I telling him that? I can have a guy over for dinner if I want to. I didn't even kiss Max, and now I never, ever would. But for some reason I hurry on. "Anyway, I'm not sure what to do. I'm scared for Doug."

"Did you call the vet?"

"Yes, and he was really nice. He checked him out, and physically, he seems okay. He said he'd call with the results of a blood test soon."

"Call him tomorrow. Tell him what happened. Maybe he can write up something about how Doug's not a dangerous dog. He has issues."

Well . . . Doug did knock Travis flat in a parking lot. But Travis seemed kind. Caring. He said he would help if he could. And I would beg him if I had to, for Doug's sake.

"Okay, good idea."

"And stay away from that Max guy. He sounds like an ass."

I agree. Although we work in the same office, I never want to see him again, and I'm sure he feels the same. How much could things change between us in one day?

"When are you coming home, Tim?" Wistful notes wind in my voice.

His shoulders tighten. "I don't *know* yet, Amelia. I still have a lot to do here. I have to get back to sleep now. Big day tomorrow with an investor."

"All right. Good night, babe. Thanks for listening." Did he just cringe when I called him babe?

"Call the vet." He leans closer to the screen. "See you, Lil' Dougie."

Doug squeaks and tries to explode out of my arms again. Tim laughs and reaches to disconnect. Just before he does, I swear the covers behind him move.

Either he learned to move at light speed . . . or someone's in his bed.

Chapter Nine

Before bed, I email Max, apologizing one more time and letting him know I'd give him a check the next morning. I don't hear anything back.

And I can't sleep for worrying. Worry about Doug, what Max will do, and . . . Tim. Did the covers on his bed really move? Was someone there? Or was I seeing things? His room was dark; I couldn't be sure. But every time I thought about it, my throat felt dry and swollen and my chest hurt.

If I told Avery, she'd remind me that Tim is free to have whoever he wants in his bed. I *know* she's right. If only my heart would accept it.

Around mid-morning the next day, I track Max out to the coffee cart in the lobby. He's leaving the register, a steaming cup in his hand. He tries to escape without speaking to me, but I corner him between a set of chairs. His eyes, once an intriguing shade of well-worn denim, now look like shards of stormy sky.

I hand him the check with trembling fingers. "Max, I'm so, so sorry about Doug. I'm sorry you were hurt, that he bit you, that—"

He holds up a hand. "I don't want your apologies. The fact is that dog is dangerous. He almost tore my flexor carpi ulnaris."

"Your . . . what?"

He doesn't stop to explain. "I can't climb for at least a month. And what if he had attacked a total stranger? Or a kid?"

My face scrunches. "We don't really have any children around."

His eyes narrow. "My point is that he could do this again, Amelia, or worse. You might be willing to live with that risk, but I'm not."

I stare at my scuffed red sandals. "What are you going to do?"

"I haven't decided. When I do, I'll let you know." He pockets the check, turns, and walks back to the elevator without another word.

"How could you do this? You're a dog owner. Don't you know how it feels?" I saw him with his black lab, Titan, at the dog park that time.

He turns and looks at me, his expression contemptuous. "Titan is my girlfriend's dog."

I can only stare. Girlfriend? As in current?

What. A. Prick.

𝄞

My first break, I head to the outdoor patio to suck down a protein shake and call the Love & Pets number.

Jo answers. "Dr. Travis is with a patient. May I take a message?"

"This is Amelia Rhodes calling about my dog, Doug. Does Travis have a voice mail where I can leave a message? It's urgent."

When my words come out waggly, Jo's voice softens. "Of course. I'll put you right through. Don't worry, honey."

"Thank you so much."

"Just a sec." Her voice disappears, replaced by instrumental music.

Travis' outgoing message says he'll return my call as soon as possible. Even recorded, his voice is so calm and reassuring, it slows my heart rate a little. I try to describe what happened without crying.

I spend the rest of my break in alternating waves of fear and anxiety. What will happen to Doug if Max reports him? If the worst happens, how can I live with myself?

Kenny stares at me when I get back. "What's going on, Princess? You look like Stinkers the time she ate a dill pickle whole."

I can't hold the tears back. Keeping my voice down, I tell Kenny what happened with Max.

He throws Max's office door a look that could wither a house-plant. "I mean, Doug shouldn't have bit him, but he doesn't need to go after him."

"Right? I feel awful that he was hurt, and I should pay his medical bills, but does he really need to threaten to . . . to . . ."

Kenny hugs me. Kenny has *never* hugged me, not even after Tim left. "We won't let that happen. I'll dig through my textbooks. Maybe I can find some way to fight Max in case he takes it there."

I blow my nose. "Thanks, Kenny. How will I survive without you when you go to CU? I love you, you know?"

"I love you, too. Now pull yourself together. Cassie's coming."

I toss the tissue and start typing. Never mind that what's ending up on the page is nonsense.

By the time I leave work, I'm starving and shaky—I felt too horrible to eat my lunch earlier—but at least I have a message back from Travis that he has a plan to help Doug.

It's 5:45 p.m. Hopefully he's still answering calls. I find a bench in the shade. His phone rings long enough that I start to bite my thumbnail.

"Amelia. From your message it sounded like Doug had an exciting weekend after I saw you."

I laugh weakly. "You could say that. My sister and I had some friends over for dinner, and Doug attacked one of them. He's threatening to have Doug" —I breathe deep—"put down."

"How bad was the injury?"

"He wouldn't really let me see, but Doug definitely broke the skin. He took himself to the ER and gave me his medical bill, which I've already paid."

He doesn't speak for a second. "Amelia, I won't act like this isn't serious. He's within his rights to press charges against you. And dogs that bite are, actually, dangerous."

"I know. I know it's serious. But . . . I can't give up on him. Do you have any ideas?"

He's quiet for a few seconds. "I've been thinking about Doug since I saw you all on Saturday, and I have a few ideas."

Hope hitches my voice up. "Like what?"

"I spoke with an animal behaviorist, a woman with a lot of experience. She said Doug sounds like he's having issues with aggression and separation anxiety."

Aggression, I can't deny. But separation anxiety? "You mean he's anxious about being away from Tim?"

"Possibly. It's a theory we can work from."

I know he misses Tim. That's obvious when we video call. But he has *me*. I take care of him, maybe even better than Tim did. I definitely spend more time with him.

"Listen, I don't make house calls often, but I'd like to come by this weekend and see Doug in his natural habitat, so to speak. With behavioral problems, it can help to narrow down the variables. The RV is a little limiting."

He barely gets the words out before I'm stammering thank you and agreeing. "You have no idea how much this means to me. I'm so scared for him. I . . . I don't know what I'd do without him."

"I'll be honest with you, Amelia, I'm not sure what I can do if the guy reports you to animal control. But I'll do my best to help Doug. How does Saturday morning sound?"

"Perfect."

I don't know what Travis can do for Doug, but for the first time since I read Max's email, the belt that's been cinched tight around my chest releases, and I can breathe.

Chapter Ten

I spend a half hour straightening the apartment before Travis comes—especially my room—while Doug lounges on my bed, chewing a rawhide bone and watching me. I even clean my bathroom, in case he has to use it.

Avery has a friend who had a home visit when she and her husband wanted to adopt a child. That's how I feel—like the home I'm providing Doug is being inspected. Is it good enough? Am *I* good enough?

The doorbell rings at ten sharp. I have to fight the urge to run and hide in my bedroom while Avery answers the door. Seriously, what is wrong with me these days? I wasn't always such a helpless coward.

"Dr. Brewer," Avery says, shaking his hand, "very nice to see you again. Thank you for coming. Amelia's about to go out of her mind."

He smiles as he greets us. "Sounds like our Doug needs some help."

Our Doug. Like he already cares about what happens to him. I can't help it. I burst into tears. Wonderful. Now what will he think about my mental health?

Avery hurries to my side. "Mel, I'm sorry. I know you're really worried. I shouldn't have teased you."

I'm sobbing so hard, I can't even tell her that's not why I'm crying. After the worst of the sobs pass, she presses a glass of water and a wad of tissue into my hand. Doug barks furiously from his crate, where I stuck him a safe ten minutes before Travis was supposed to arrive.

"I'm sorry. I'm such a disaster these days," I say as the tears slow. I drink to control the hiccups I feel coming.

Travis touches my shoulder. "Amelia, you love your pet, and you're worried about him. What's so disastrous about that?"

I go to the kitchen to blow my nose and drink the water, taking a little time to compose myself. I can hear Avery whispering to Travis while I'm gone.

When I return, he asks, "Can I see where Doug stays?"

I wave him toward my room. "This way."

Travis keeps his eyes on Doug in the crate as he goes in. I guess I didn't need to clean up after all.

"Hey, Doug. How're you doing, buddy?" Travis asks, while Doug bares his teeth and growls.

"Doug," I say, but Travis interrupts.

"No worries, Amelia. He's obviously a territorial kind of guy. He knows what's his, and he wants to protect it." His eyes hold mine for a second, before he gestures to my desk chair. "May I?"

"Of course."

He puts his forearms on his legs and leans forward to study Doug. "Is he in his crate while you're gone from the apartment?"

I nod and frown. "Lately, yes. He used to be okay to hang out while we worked, but he's destroyed too many things the last few months. The couch, the coffee table, oh, he ate almost a whole bag of Starbucks French roast, and I've had to replace practically all of my underwear." I stop as my cheeks get hot. "Doug . . . likes to eat them."

Travis raises an eyebrow. "Who can blame him?"

I laugh, but that strange moth is loose in my chest again.

"I've been running home at lunch to walk him when I can, but my bosses aren't very understanding when I'm late getting back. I spend a lot of time with him when I'm not working, too." And now, in addition to talking to him about my underwear, I'm telling him I have no social life. Better and better.

"Does he have other quirks?"

"Quirks?" I ask.

"Other than eating underwear and being suspicious of men, I mean."

Avery speaks from the doorway. "Play the song for him, Mel."

I turn around with a questioning look, and she nods at me encouragingly.

"I guess this is the biggest one."

I pull up "Girl, I Love You So Bad" on my phone and play it through the portable speaker on my bedside table.

As he hears the beginning notes, Doug stands stock still to listen. He starts to quiver, then howl, and finally, to throw himself into the bars of the cage. Travis watches, his expression unreadable.

After a minute, I stop the music, and Doug stops, too. His chubby sides puff in and out as he breathes. I want to open the cage and comfort him, but I don't dare with Travis here.

"It's my"—I glance at Avery—"*ex*-boyfriend's favorite song. He used to play the song, then give Doug treats when he'd come running. It never made him react like this before, but since Tim left . . ." I hold my hands up.

Travis nods. "I can see what you're up against."

How can he sound like he *truly* knows?

He sits back. "My guess is Doug's experiencing separation anxiety, like my colleague suggested." He glances at the framed selfie of Tim and me, heads together and smiling next to the speaker on my bedside table. Remembering the day we took it steals my breath. He told me he loved me that day.

I tear my eyes away to find Travis watching me. He doesn't seem to miss much. When he speaks, his voice is gentle.

"When dogs display this kind of behavior, we have to teach them that it's safe for them to be by themselves, that they're okay without the person they're separated from."

My heart thumps in a weird way. *"How* do we do that?"

"Getting him comfortable around other men would be most helpful, but we probably shouldn't risk that, given his aggression." He pauses. "He might get similar benefits from spending more time around other dogs, though."

Avery speaks up again. "How do you know he won't attack them, too?"

"We'll take it slow. I have a connection with a pug rescue organization. I could get in touch and see if Brenda might be willing to allow Doug to visit. What do you think?"

Doug whines. He hasn't taken his eyes off Travis since he arrived.

My insides squirm with nerves. Is this a good idea? Can Doug handle it? Or will it end with someone else being hurt? I don't know, but this is why I called Travis for help in the first place. I have to try something.

"Let's do it."

Travis stands, startling Doug, who barks.

"Great. I'll give her a call and let you know what she says."

"I hate to ask," Avery says, "but how much will all this cost?"

I wince, but she's right to ask. I don't have a ton of extra funds, especially after paying for Max's ER visit. Tim will help pay for Doug's treatment, but sometimes he doesn't reimburse me quickly enough for me to pay my credit card bill. I know it's because he's out of the country, although Avery reminds me PayPal takes a few seconds at most.

"Why don't we see how much time this ends up taking?" Travis says.

"I wouldn't feel right not paying you up front," I say.

"All right, if it makes you feel better, I'll come up with a flat fee."

I agree, and we walk him to the door.

"Thank you so much for helping us," I say.

"You're very welcome."

That full-mouth smile—it transforms his face. Dazzled, I block the door, and Avery has to poke me in the back to get me to move. I shake myself and hold the door for him.

"See you soon," he says.

I watch him move down the hall before shutting the door. The way he walks is smooth, athletic, confident without being cocky.

When I turn back, Avery's leaning against the wall wearing a small smile.

"What?" I ask.

"Nothing. Nothing at all."

Chapter Eleven

Travis calls about an hour before I get off work. Kenny covers me so I can sneak out and talk to him from a stall in the women's restroom. Cassie's already gone for the day.

"Saturday morning works to introduce you and Doug to my contact at the pug rescue." He sounds upbeat.

I melt with relief. "Great! What time?"

"Eleven o'clock. I'll block my schedule right now."

"Wait—you're going too?"

"I thought I would, if you don't mind. I'd like to see how it goes to decide if this is the course we should take with Doug."

Although the idea of seeing Dr. Travis Brewer again is far from unappealing, I hesitate. "But . . . that seems like going above and beyond."

"I like to think I go the extra mile for my patients."

"Well, if you're sure, then thank you. Where's the rescue?"

"In Bennett, out east, on the plains, so about a forty-five-minute drive."

"I don't have a car, but I can get a Lyft." It costs a fortune to get to the airport, and that's only about halfway, but this is important.

"Why don't I pick you up?"

"No, that's too much trouble. I can get there."

"Not at all. Happy to do it."

The thing is, he *sounds* happy to do it, too. His offer is really generous but . . . almost an hour each way in the Love & Pets RV with him? What will we talk about? Why is he doing this?

"I'm emailing you an invoice with my fee. If it's a burden, call me and we'll work out a payment plan."

"Okay, thanks again. I'll see you Saturday."

We hang up, and I find his invoice: $150. The initial appointment cost more. Is this a scam? Is he a serial killer who lures women by offering to drive them out to the plains to visit pug rescues? Or . . . does he actually care?

I told Travis I'd meet him on the sidewalk in front of my building. Manuel waves to me from his office as I go by but side-eyes Doug, who's muzzled. I brought Manuel homemade cookies and an apology card, so I'm back in his good graces, but clearly Doug isn't.

I'm expecting a wall of turquoise blue to pull down the street, so I don't notice at first when Travis pulls up in an older, dark green SUV. He waves and reaches over to open the passenger door for me. I pop Doug in the back seat and jump in. I expect him to act up when he sees and smells Travis, but miraculously, he sniffs around for a minute, then lies down, quiet.

"I thought you'd be in the RV," I say as we pull away from the curb.

"She works hard all week, like Jo and me, so I like to give her weekends off. Plus, she's a bitch to park."

I laugh. "I'll bet."

He smiles, and I feel that flutter again. He looks amazing in scrubs, but the T-shirt and jeans he's wearing today hug his body in all the right places.

I'd prepared myself for an hour of awkward silence, but we fall into easy conversation as he drives us north on I-25 to eastbound I-

70. The Colorado sky is clear and sunny, showcasing the jagged peaks of the mountains in the distance, and Saturday-morning traffic isn't bad at all. Doug might have a chance at getting better. Somehow, our ride out to Bennett feels like an adventure. Pathetic, I know, but I'll take what I can get.

Travis tells me about a few of his patients, including a constipated bearded dragon, filing the ever-growing teeth of a rat who was too old to gnaw them down herself, and a visit out to an urban farm to check on a pregnant goat.

"You sound like you love your work." Can he hear the jealousy in my voice?

"Love it. My grandmother always tells me I was born to be a veterinarian. She says *dog* was one of the first words I spoke, and I was always treating some stuffed animal or another in my pretend clinic." He smiles, but it's not as bright.

"Is she still living?" I ask.

He nods. "You met her, actually."

"Jo? Jo's your grandmother?"

"One and the same. Her name's Josephine, but I've only ever called her Jo. She's been a vet tech for almost thirty years. When I graduated from vet school, it was her idea to start the mobile clinic together. Low overhead, more variety of work. And . . . she lives with me, too. So yeah, we get plenty of time together."

I turn all the way to face him. "No way. You live with your grandmother?"

I've never heard of a man my age living and working with his grandmother. But after meeting Jo and talking to her a few times, I can see why Travis does.

"Technically, she lives with me. She had her own place until recently, but I checked on her most evenings anyway once she started treatment, so it made more sense to have her move in. Hopefully it's only temporary."

"Treatment?"

His grip on the wheel tightens. "Lung cancer. She'd probably still have a cigarette or two a day if I didn't watch her like a hawk."

That cough she had and how frail she looked . . . "I'm so sorry. How is she doing?"

"As well as can be expected. She's still able to work, although she has a pretty laid back boss. If she needs to stay home and rest, she doesn't get fired." He flashes a smile.

"So . . . you're single?" Ugh, it just popped out. I flush. "I'm sorry. None of my business."

"It's okay." He glances out the side window as another small cloud passes over his face. "I was engaged a while ago. It didn't work out."

I'm curious about what happened, but I've pried enough. I've already asked Travis five more questions than I managed to come up with for Max. Out the window, the city is speeding by, slowing exchanging apartment buildings for suburbs.

Maybe one more. "Do you have pets?" That was a safe question, right? Not too invasive.

"Ten."

My jaw drops. "Ten pets? What are they?"

"Let's see." He taps each finger against the wheel, counting. "Four dogs, two cats—although the cats are Jo's—a handful of leopard frogs that I count as one, a whiptail lizard, a cranky sunbeam snake, and a bison named Chuck."

My eyes widen. "Where do you live, the zoo?"

He pulls a face. "Might as well."

"And I thought I had problems with one miserable pug."

He laughs. "Oh, our Doug does have problems, no doubt, but we're going to work on those." He checks his blind spot and switches lanes. "So let me tell you a little more about the rescue we're going to. The woman who runs it, Brenda, gets pugs from all over the country and adopts them out, sometimes driving them days to a new home. She's really great and really caring, but she's . . . eccentric."

"In what way?"

"I'll let you see for yourself."

I look back at Doug and feel sick with worry again. Travis must see it on my face.

"Try not to stress, Amelia. We'll figure this out."

We. We'll figure this out. *Our* Doug.

I dig in my bag. "Before I forget, I have a check for you. The invoice was just for today, right? I still owe you for the house call?"

He shrugs. "We'll call it good at $150."

"But you aren't charging enough."

"I've been accused of that before. It's okay, really. I don't do this work for the money. I genuinely want to see Doug improve. I love animals, and I get a lot of joy out of helping them and their owners."

I blink. "Joy?"

"Yeah." Humor flits over his face. "Haven't you ever met someone who gets joy from their work?"

"Um, not really, no." Or at least not anyone who would admit to it.

"Try working with animals." He snaps his fingers. "Instant joy."

Maybe so, but I'm most intrigued that he admits it. What kind of guy is Travis Brewer, anyway?

A few minutes later, he checks his mirror as he exits the interstate and takes the overpass, heading north. In a blink we're through the little town of Bennett, and he turns off on a dirt road, bouncing us closer to a small ranch in the distance. As dust curls around the SUV, I realize it was a good thing he picked me up. No Lyft driver in her right mind would have brought me all the way here.

At the end of the ranch's driveway is a sign. I read it. "Pug Paradise?"

"Didn't I tell you that's what Brenda's place is called? Welcome to paradise, Amelia and Doug."

The ranch house is—was—white. Some of the roof tiles are gone, and a wood porch droops off the front. An ancient truck lazes over to the side. Toward the back of the house is a good-sized shed, or maybe small barn, that looks in better repair.

But what really catches my eye is the person standing out front, a hand held to her eyes to shade them from the sun. She's dressed in some sort of costume: golden-colored with a black hood and . . . ears.

"Is that—?"

"Brenda." Travis glances at me. "Don't say I didn't warn you."

"But she's wearing a—"

"Yeah. It's a pug suit."

Chapter Twelve

I almost burst out laughing, but we're close enough that Brenda can see me, so I stop myself. My throat hurts with the effort.

"Travis, that's a few stops past quirky," I say.

He shrugs and pulls out that slow grin. "I try not to judge."

He parks his car beside Brenda's truck, and we get out to greet her. I help Doug out of the back. He whines in an unsettled way. Still, he's being pretty quiet—for Doug.

Only the woman's face is visible in the pug suit, but I can tell she's well into her sixties. Her skin is tanned and wrinkled, like a dried apple. Bushy gray eyebrows frame light brown eyes, and her teeth are yellowed. When she speaks, her voice is short and sharp, almost a bark.

"Well. Travis. What kind of mischief have you brought me now?"

"No French bulldogs this time, Brenda."

They both guffaw, leaving me feeling like I missed the joke, but I laugh anyway. It's kind of infectious. He gives her a hug, then turns to me.

"Brenda, I'd like you to meet Amelia and her dog, Doug."

She nods to me but her eyes are on Doug. "Let me get a look at this little man." She squats smoothly for an older woman.

"Careful." I pull him away. "Doug's not very . . . he can be aggressive." Not usually with women, but Doug looks as mystified by Brenda and her costume as I am.

At least he's not going ballistic. I hope it doesn't mean he's plotting his attack.

Brenda narrows her eyes as she studies him and nods knowingly. "Hello there, Douglas. What do you say we take you to see my puglets?"

She turns and without another word disappears around the side of house, heading toward the shed.

Travis raises his eyebrows, like *told you*, and tips his head that way. "After you."

"Are you sure she's okay?" I ask him in a whisper. My hand brushes his as we walk, and a tiny bolt of lightning passes between us. I shiver, but I can't tell if he feels it, too.

"As okay as a woman in a dog suit can be." But he watches Brenda with an indulgent expression. Sniffing the air, Doug strains against his leash and pulls me forward.

In front of the shed-barn is a grassy area surrounded by a fence. Brenda steps through the gate, closes it behind her, and bellows. "Puglets? Where are you?"

A chorus of shrill barks greet her yell. From inside the shed, a gaggle of pugs come running. They're about the same shape as Doug—and Brenda—and every size in between. Some are tan, like Doug, and others are black. A couple are a mix—brindle, I think it's called. Dark eyes trained on Brenda, they hop up on her legs or run around her, barking and whining.

Doug freezes, listening and watching. His ears are erect. I can't hear him, but his teeth show in a growl. I pick him up and kiss his head, shushing him. He smells like he needs a bath.

"Are you going to put him in with them?" I ask Brenda nervously.

"Mercy, no. Not yet. That would be like throwing a chicken to crocodiles. They don't know each other yet. With aggression issues, you've got to move slow. Today is just about letting them get used to each other's scents."

Relieved, I set Doug down again, and we walk a little closer to the fence. Travis stands beside me. He has that pleasant, slightly salty smell people have after they've been in the sun for a while. It's not sweat yet. It's . . . sunshine. I lean a smidge closer to breathe him in.

Brenda putters around the area talking to the pugs, checking several water bowls that sit in the shady area, and with a bucket and shovel, scooping poop. The pugs—I count six of them—prance around her, tussling and playing with one another. Two of them chase each other. One small pup chews on another's ear. The whole scene might be the most adorable thing I've ever seen.

"All of these pugs are rescues?" I ask Travis.

"They are. Pug Paradise is well known around the country. If you have an abandoned pug, or extras from a puppy mill, call Brenda."

I lower my voice. "Why does she wear that outfit?"

He lifts a shoulder. "She says it helps her rescues feel more comfortable with her. A lot of them come from less than ideal circumstances. They're freaked out when they get here. When she's not wearing the suit, she lets them sleep with it, like a security blanket. She says it helps them adjust to being here until they can be adopted or fostered. Actually, that's not a bad idea for you."

I raise an eyebrow. "You think I should wear a pug suit?"

He tugs on the sleeve of my shirt. "Sure. Shouldn't everyone?" The backs of his fingers linger against my skin for a second. "No, I mean put something in Doug's crate that smells like you. It could help him feel less stressed during the day." He points to the shed. "Anyway, you should see in there. *Brenda's* house might be a wreck, but *their* place is pristine. She calls it the hotel. Only the finest food and chew toys. Heat in the winter and air-conditioning in the summer. If she doesn't get enough donations to pay for it, she covers it, even though she's on a fixed income. Don't worry, these dogs are spoiled."

Brenda walks back over. "Well. Mind giving these puglets a once over, Dr. Travis?"

"You bet." He heads toward the gate.

"Can I help?" I ask.

Brenda shakes her pug head. "Not today. You should stay with Douglas. With us in here, maybe you can take that muzzle off for a while. But if he acts up, back on it goes."

Travis goes into the fenced area and greets the pugs. One drops on its back and squirms, just like Doug. When he's safely inside, I pull Doug's muzzle off.

"Will you be a good boy?"

He's not even looking at me. The pugs have captured his attention. I sit beside the fence and keep him in my lap. His tail and ears are up, and his muscles are so tense he quivers, but he makes no sound. He really hasn't been around many dogs, I realize. And the only people he sees regularly are Avery, Jason, and me. I guess his socialization *has* sucked.

While Brenda and Travis disappear inside the shed with one of the pugs, the others play. One big guy lies in the shade, panting. A much smaller one, a female, jogs right up to us. Her wrinkled head tips to the side, and she whines, her eyes on Doug.

He stands, but I keep him close. Even with the fence between them, I don't trust him. The girl pug's pink tongue suddenly hangs out of her mouth, giving her an especially friendly expression. And . . . Doug looks smitten.

"You can let him approach the fence," Brenda says, poking her head out. "But keep a good grip on his leash."

I bite my lip. He can't hurt her, but I hate it when he loses control and goes berserk. Still, we came all this way. We have to start somewhere. I let him move closer.

The girl pug comes near enough to the fence to touch her nose to it. Doug stays still. Then he charges forward. I jerk the leash back.

"Relax," Brenda says. "I can tell you're scared from over here, so you can bet he knows it, too."

I take a deep breath and relax the leash. Doug moves a foot closer. He's inches from the fence now. Slowly, his curly tail wags. The girl pug's tail wags back. Their noses touch through the fence. My shoulders relax, and I smile.

Until another dog rushes over, eager to see Doug, and he loses it, barking and snarling. All the pugs come running, and he gets even louder and more vicious-sounding. Heart pounding, I pull him back, inch by inch, and fit the muzzle back on his face, like Brenda said to do. Travis comes to the fence.

"You okay?" he asks.

"I'm fine, just disappointed. It was going so well for a second there."

"That wasn't a bad start at all," Brenda says. "A lot of my abused dogs carry on like that at first, and they're part of the pack in no time."

"Abused?" I say, stung. "Doug's not abused."

"No, but he acts the same. Suspicious. Angry. Maybe heartbroken. These dogs may not be able to express it the same way, but they feel some of the same emotions we do."

Heartbroken. I stare at my sandals and swallow. When I look up again, Travis is studying me with a sympathetic smile.

"At least now we know who Douglas's ambassador will be next time. Daisy's taken a shine to him, and him to her."

I blink. "Daisy? What a cute name for a pug."

"Well. It was on her collar when they found her in Nebraska, but the phone number was disconnected. Never could find her owners. She's a sweet potato pie, that one."

Travis heads back to the pugs. He does a quick examination of each one, checking out their ears, eyes, and nose with one of those pointy lighted medical instruments, telling Brenda anything she might want to keep an eye on. He has to do Daisy's exam right there in front of us because of her fascination with Doug.

"I'm going to help Brenda out with a few things in the hotel," Travis says.

I let Doug's leash go slack and, eyes closed, look up at the sun.

It feels warm and wonderful, and I open up to it like . . . a daisy. Doug's calm reaction to Daisy, while not much, gives me hope for the first time since he trapped Manuel in the bedroom. I wasn't sure how meeting a bunch of pugs could help, but maybe Brenda knows what she's doing, pug suit and all.

When Travis finishes, he washes his hands at a pump and comes out of the gate. The pugs gather behind him, tails wagging. Brenda stays inside. Doug peers through the gate at the others, his tail and ears relaxed.

"He looks a lot more comfortable now," I say.

Brenda pushes her pug face back, wipes a trickle of sweat off her temple, and beams. Her sun-pinked skin has a field of freckles across it. "He did good. Next time we might try letting him in with the others."

I shake her, er, paw. "Thank you so much for letting us visit, Brenda. Pug Paradise is amazing."

"Well. You're very welcome, Amelia. I'll see you both soon." She waves at Doug. "Now you behave yourself, young man."

"Don't forget about the Love & Pets Party," Travis says to Brenda. "August twenty-fourth."

"Wouldn't dream of it." She winks.

Travis hums along to the radio, a country music station, as we cruise back toward Denver. Doug is quiet.

"Everything okay?" Travis asks.

I startle. "What?"

"You made a face."

How did he see that? He wasn't even looking at me. "I was thinking about work."

"I'm sorry."

"About what?"

"That thinking about work makes you make a face."

I sigh loudly. "No work joy for me."

He chuckles. His black hair gleams in the sun, but something golden is stuck in his short, messy ponytail. Without thinking, I reach over and pluck it out, then hold it up as he throws me a questioning look.

"Straw." Instead of dropping it, I keep it, rolling it between my fingers. "So what's the party you mentioned to Brenda?"

"It's an idea I've had for a while," he says. "A community fair to help low-income folks vaccinate and get basic veterinary services for their pets for free or low cost. Jo and I have been planning it for a few months, trying to get sponsors, permits from the city, that kind of thing. But she hasn't felt well enough to work on it lately, so I'm behind."

I lick my lips. "I . . . I could help you."

He glances over.

My words spill out faster, chased by nerves. "I mean, I'm pretty free on weekends, and I'm not even that busy at work. Half the time I'm on Instagram or looking up recipes because I don't have enough to do. You've been so nice about helping Doug, and you're barely charging me, so I'd be happy to help. Really."

He thinks about it for a minute, then nods. "Thanks, Amelia. I'd appreciate that. Jo and I are having a planning session tomorrow if you'd like to join us?"

"Sure."

He smiles. We have these night storms in Colorado sometimes, where lightning flashes silently behind the clouds, lighting up the sky in spectacular ways. That's how his touch feels to me. Sparks fly through my veins, and my mouth goes dry.

Behind us, Doug makes a noise that sounds suspiciously like a cross between a growl and a sigh.

Chapter Thirteen

I thought a veterinarian who has ten animals would live on an overgrown lot off some two-lane road with a neglected house and a motorcycle or three-wheeler parked in the driveway. Sort of like the male version of Brenda.

But as I pull up at Travis's house in Avery's car to help plan the community fair, it's nothing like it. Well, other than being off a two-lane road.

Instead, there's a freshly painted A-frame home with wood trim, a wide and inviting porch, and roses. Two trimmed rows of all colors from hot pink to deep red preen on either side of the porch. Although I suspect Jo had a hand in planting or at least tending those.

A sturdy fence outlines a dirt paddock that I can barely see from the driveway. As I park beside Travis's SUV and get out, the front door opens. Four dogs bark and run my way. One looks like a feisty terrier, one's some kind of jowly hound, and I'm pretty sure the big one is a pony in disguise. The fourth one, a little mutt, trots more than runs, tail wagging.

Jo comes out the door behind them, whistling surprisingly loudly for someone so tiny and frail. Now that I see her again, I realize that Travis might as well be a tracing of her, only taller, sturdier, and definitely more male.

"Amelia?" Jo calls, her voice breathy. "Don't worry about the Horsemen. They're just a loud welcome committee."

Sure enough, the dogs carve crazy circles around my feet but don't jump on me or growl. The terrier leaps so high and excitedly that he falls on his back, barking as he rights himself.

Jo hangs on the handrail as she moves down each step. She's carrying a portable oxygen tank with a strap over her shoulder, and clear tubing stretches around her neck and into her nostrils from the machine. But her shower of gray hair is glorious against a thin turquoise fleece.

I hurry to her side, minding the pooches. "Can I help?"

"You can shake my hand." She holds hers out, a smile brightening her face. Her skin feels papery, her bones too light. "Thank you for helping my Travis. This event means so much to him."

Jo has the same defined cheekbones and brow as Travis, although her eye color is more hazel than dark brown, like his. But the warmth in them is identical to her grandson's.

I hug her gently. "I'm glad to help."

"Hey." Travis stands behind me, at the corner of the house. He's wearing jeans, a dark green work shirt, and hiking boots. His hair is pulled back again with pieces loose around his face, and dirt smudges his neck. He could have rolled in mud and he'd still look amazing.

"You've met Jo." He smiles at his grandmother. "And these canine disasters are the Four Horsemen."

"Like—of the Apocalypse?"

"When they all get excited, it's like war, famine, death, and conquest rolled into one." He points to each dog from biggest to smallest. "This is Luke, Cooper, Oliver, and Dex."

Jo takes my arm. "I read on the internet recently that almost fifty percent of dogs are named human names. Did you know that?" Her eyes are bright as she speaks, but she leans on me as we walk, and her breathing is uneven. "My cats are Peanut Butter and Jelly. I call them PB and J." She laughs, then coughs.

I chuckle, too. "Were you hungry when you named them?"

"Probably. I always am. Well, used to be."

Travis takes his grandmother's arm, his movements gentle. He smiles tenderly. "Doing okay?"

She waves her hand. "I'm fine, I'm fine. Don't fuss over me." She points to the paddock. "Why don't you introduce Amelia to Chuck? I'll go pour us some iced tea."

Travis walks Jo to the door and opens it for her, the Horsemen at their heels. She steps in slowly, and his smile fades as he returns to me.

"She isn't fine, is she?" I ask quietly.

"I don't think so. It felt like her oncologist was telling me to prepare myself this week at her appointment." His tall frame shrinks several inches as his shoulders hunch and his head bows. The dogs sit at his feet, and the terrier, Oliver, whines.

I lay a hand on his back. "I'm sorry, Travis. She seems like a really sweet lady."

He doesn't speak for almost a full minute. I keep my hand where it is, feeling his shallow breathing as he tries to contain his emotions. I wish I knew what else to say.

When he looks up, his eyes glitter like dark jewels. "Let's meet Chuck."

We walk toward the fence where the bison waits. He's massive, with thick wavy fur around his shoulders, a humped back, and a thin tail with a tuft of hair at the end. His muscular legs end in cloven hooves that look sharp enough to cut skin.

"Chuck, this is Amelia." The humor that's usually in Travis's voice is back.

"Nice to meet you." I hold out my hand as if to shake the closest of the curved horns on either side of his head, but Travis grabs my fingers.

"Careful. He isn't as friendly as he likes to pretend. If you got inside his fence, he'd make you run a forty-yard dash for time—or else. Worse than a middle-school gym teacher."

Thanks to Travis's hand holding mine, and the sparkly feeling that suddenly shoots through my body, I have to unscramble my thoughts before I can say anything intelligible.

"How . . . how did you end up with a bison?"

He puts his hand in his pocket. "In about the same way as Brenda gets her pugs. He was found, skinny and neglected, on a ramshackle ranch in west Texas. Chuck can defend himself, but he can't grow his own food or fetch water. A rancher here in Colorado tried to incorporate him into his herd, but he didn't get along with the others. He was on his way to being euthanized, so I adopted him. We have an understanding. Right, boy?"

Travis clucks his tongue at the animal. Chuck's nostrils spread as he lifts his head and snorts in what I swear is an affectionate way.

I eye his solid body. "He has to be expensive to feed."

"True. You hungry, Chuck?" Travis reaches into a wide container outside the fence and pulls out a handful of what looks like straw or prairie grass. Travis thrusts the grass in where the bison can reach it. Chuck's dark lips draw it toward rows of straight, white teeth, and he gets to munching.

"Is that all he eats?" I ask.

"This guy is 100 percent grass fed. Timothy grass is his favorite, and he likes bluegrass, ryegrass, and fescue. But," he lowers his voice conspiratorially, "clover is his guilty pleasure."

I picture Chuck with a mouthful of four-leaf clover and smile.

"Want to give him some?" Travis asks.

"Yes!"

He hands me a handful of grass from the container. When Chuck finishes his mouthful, I offer the grass to him. I've never been this close to a bison before, much less fed one.

Travis stares at Chuck, his expression pinched. "There were twenty to thirty million of these animals in North America at one time. By the late 1800s, they were down to one thousand."

"And now?"

"Now there are about half a million. It's better than a thousand, but still. Humans are the worst kinds of predators." His voice is bitter. He glances at me, and his face relaxes a little.

"Sorry," he says. "It's been a rough day with Jo. And . . . I get a little carried away about this stuff."

"Don't apologize for your passion." I think of Tim. He's just as passionate about basketball. "I wish I had more of it."

"No passion in there, huh?" Travis nudges me with a cheeky smile.

My face feels like I stuck it in a fryer. "No. Yes! I mean, I wish I cared more about . . . good causes."

"Hey, don't be too hard on yourself." His voice is soft. "You're here to help me with one, right?"

I nod. How does he manage to know exactly what to say to help me feel better? I swallow.

"Speaking of, we should get started," he says.

I follow him inside. The front door opens into a sunny living room with a TV, worn but comfy-looking couch, and a pair of chairs. PB and J are curled up in the chairs like they own them, barely glancing up as we come in. The Four Horsemen run to greet us. In the corner, an aquarium holds what looks like a miniature jungle, complete with a mini volcano. Given that he takes care of so many animals, Travis's house is surprisingly neat and clean.

Jo sits at the table, one hand wrapped around a glass of tea, the other cradling her chin. She's staring out the window, but a smile lifts the lines of her face as Travis and I enter.

"Tea?" Jo asks me. I thank her as she hands me a glass.

"Here are a few more of the gang." Travis points to the aquarium. "These are the spotted leopard frogs—I haven't really named them because I can't keep them straight—and Leo, the whiptail lizard." The frogs hop around, but Leo—his tail thin like a whip—sits very still in a corner.

Travis picks up a jar and shakes it over the aquarium. Tiny black crickets fall in and hop around wildly. A couple of the frogs freeze, then quick as a gunshot, their tongues lash out. At least one gets lucky.

I wrinkle my nose. "That's kinda gross."

Travis shrugs. "A frog's gotta eat. You get used to it."

I peer in, trying to ignore the crickets getting slurped up. "Is the snake in there, too?"

Travis waves a hand. "Oh, Sunny's around somewhere."

I clutch his arm. "Wait, seriously? You let it slither around your house?"

"Sure. She helps with the mouse problem."

"Mice?" My voice jumps an octave.

He puts a comforting arm around me. "Just messing with you. Sunny has a big tank in the guest room. I let her out for exercise, but not with visitors around."

He squeezes my shoulder, his grip warm and firm, and I blush. Jo watches us. Sick or not, she doesn't seem to miss any more than her grandson does. She pulls out the chair beside her and pats it. "Come have a seat, Amelia, and I'll show you what we're working on."

Oxygen machine beside her, her voice rasping, she gives me an overview of the fair.

"Travis will be there with the Love & Pets-mobile, of course, doing free checkups and low-cost vaccinations. For fun, we'll have booths centered around pets, like a local raw dog food company, a woman who hand-sews pet beds to order, and groomers on-site; and booths for humans, like a face painter, balloon artist, and food trucks. We're calling it the first annual Love & Pets Party."

She sounds proud, as if she came up with the name. Travis sits on my other side, opens a dented laptop, and navigates to a checklist.

"We've got the date set, we reserved the park, and we have a few sponsors. We could really use more though. And we need to get some advertising going, book a few food trucks, arrange a DJ for music, find a face painter for the kids, those kinds of things."

Joe taps her pen on the table. "I've been calling around to as many local pet businesses as I can. A few are interested, but they haven't committed yet."

"I'm working on the advertising, social media, and updating our website," Travis says.

"I get Doug's food at a cute natural pet store downtown. I can ask them to sponsor." I think about it. "And I know someone who owns a food truck, Benny's Bodacious Bowls." Benny was a guy I met through Tim. "I can ask if he can make it on that date, and maybe he has some food-truck friends who'd want in. Oh—and our local ice cream shop, Bovine Divine, has a truck on weekends, too. I'll ask them. I'm sure I can find a face painter and balloon artist."

Travis opens a different document and shows me the budget. "Yeah, it's not huge. So if you can get a friend discount for anything we need to pay for, even better." He leans back and rests an arm on the back of my chair. "This has been a dream of mine for a while. I can't wait to see it come together."

I tip my head to the side. "What inspired the idea?"

"I work with a lot of owners who sometimes have to choose between feeding their kids and treating their pets. I'd like to make this an annual event, so people can count on their basic pet care being covered every year."

I study him. I've met people who love their work, their sport, or some other interest, but Travis has a quiet intensity about him that tells me this passion burns especially deep.

I pull out my cell phone. "Then let's get to work."

Two hours later, I'm in the backyard with Chuck, making one last phone call to a foodie friend of Benny's. I'd managed to get Benny to commit to the date, I booked the Bovine Divine truck, and I left messages for several face painters and balloon artists. I called the pet store where I shop and a few other places about sponsorships, too. Chuck watches me balefully while I wrap up the call.

Travis joins me, and I tell him what I've done and my plan for the week. He looks impressed.

"What do you mean you don't care? You're a force of nature." He puts a hand on my shoulder. It's a hot afternoon, but when he touches me, it feels like a sun flare hit the Earth. "Thank you, Amelia. Your help means a lot to me."

His hair is glossy in the sun. I want to touch it, to feel its texture, but I don't dare.

"I have an idea. I'm doing rounds next Saturday in the RV. Would you want to come help out? Jo's just not up to it." He hurries to add, "I'd pay you for your time, of course."

"You don't need to pay me." I smile. "I'm in."

Chapter Fourteen

It's exceptionally hard to focus at work the next week. Every time I make an appointment for a client, laugh at one of Jim's stupid jokes, or catch sight of Max—which is at least once an hour—I find myself thinking about Travis. His laugh, his smile, his electric touch. How gentle he is with Jo, how much he cares about his animals—his own and other people's.

At least it keeps my thoughts off Max's threat. As I daydream, Max stops by the desk to talk to Kenny. I study him in my peripheral vision. His arm seems fine now. At least, he moves it well. I tried to ask him how he was, but he acted like I didn't even speak. If he absolutely has to tell me something, he emails me. Suits me, but I want to know if he's going to do anything about Doug. Why hasn't he said anything else? Has he decided not to report him, or is he enjoying tormenting me by saying nothing at all? If that's his strategy, it's working.

Ugh. How did I ever think he was good-looking?

After Max walks away, Kenny's eyes narrow. "That man is hot as July, but I definitely won't miss seeing him when I leave, now that I know what he's really like."

I wince. "Please don't talk about leaving."

He sighs. "Princess, it's coming soon."

I stick my fingers in my ears and hum. *Now* who's being immature? I drop my arms and make a face. "But we'll see each other, right? We'll go out for drinks sometimes, like we talked about?"

"Of course. But you know I'll be—"

"Studying, I know. Oh Kenny, I'm really going to miss you." I lower my voice. "You're the only thing that makes working here bearable."

He turns to me, crosses his arms, and cocks his head. "Then maybe you should think about working somewhere else."

I toy with my tea mug. The little hearts I painted on the sides months ago with *T+A* in them are starting to wear away, and tiny cracks run through the fired ceramic. "I know, but . . . I don't know what else I want to do."

He turns to his keyboard and types something, then pushes his monitor my way. A job search site pops up. "Only one way to find out."

I know I should start looking for another job. I've felt paralyzed since Tim left. Volunteering to help Travis was the first thing I really *wanted* to do in so long. And now I get to ride along with him on his rounds. For the first time in months, I'm looking forward to something other than Tim's call, and it feels . . . good.

❧

Travis picks me up early Saturday morning in the Love & Pets RV.

I'm wearing my favorite jeans, sneakers, and bright blue baseball hat with the Colorado flag on it that Avery says brings out the blue in my eyes. Not on purpose or anything. Definitely not.

"Morning." Travis greets me with a smile that warms my heart and downright melts other parts of me. "How's Doug?"

I sigh. "He's . . . okay."

Actually, he's been in a foul mood for the past week, and he's scorned my attempts to cheer him up. It was almost as if he smelled Travis all over me when I got home from his house last weekend, and he hasn't forgiven me.

He went on a hunger strike the first few days, forcing me to hand-feed him. This morning, I had to roll him off my pillow like a hot dog out of a bun to get him going, and then he sat down halfway through his walk and refused go any farther, making me carry him. He only cheered up when Tim called last night.

I frown. Huh. My heart didn't do the funny little skip it usually does when I think of Tim's face on my screen.

"What's up?" Travis says.

Whatever I was going to say gets stuck in my throat. It's so unfair how handsome he looks, even in scrubs. Today's set is light green and sets off his creamy tan skin.

I wave a hand. "Doug's being a pain, but that's nothing new. Where are we headed first?"

He glances in the side mirror and pulls into the right lane, ready to merge onto I-25 North.

"Coal Creek Canyon, south of Boulder. I have a client there with ninety-nine problems. Thankfully I'm not one of them." He winks.

"What kind of problems?" *Please don't let it be mice or rats.*

"The feline variety. Calling Beatrix a cat lady is an understatement."

"Beatrix? That's an unusual name."

"She said her mom was a big fan of Peter Rabbit."

We chat about our week as the RV rolls north and west toward the foothills. Travis's work was a lot more interesting than mine. He saw everything from tortoises to horses to an ornery, and illegal, pet prairie dog. Me? I cleaned out Cassie's file cabinets and did eight hours' worth of shredding. Yay.

The mountains grow larger as we travel closer, their peaks summer-brown and bare of snow. The sun shows the details of them, including the Flatirons, three peaks shaped like upright irons that define Boulder's landscape. Along with a little promontory of rock called Devil's Thumb.

"You know what people call Devil's Thumb, right?" I'm sure he already knows.

He stares blankly back and shakes his head. "No. What?"

My eyes grow wide. Tim told me, but Travis grew up here. How could he not know? "Oh. Um. Well, it's kind of crude."

He shakes his head. "Okay. What is it? What do they call it?"

"You know the shape of it. It's like a thumb, but it's also like . . . you know . . . another body part.

His expression is innocent. "Which one?"

My shoulders sag. Ugh. Why did I bring this up? "Penis Peak! They call it Penis Peak."

A sly look steals over his face. "No kidding."

My eyes narrow. "You already knew." He laughs, his Adam's apple bobbing. I smack him lightly on the arm.

Coal Creek Canyon zigs and zags into the foothills alongside a stream cascading out of the high country. Craggy slopes rise on either side of the two-lane road dotted with pine trees and gaggles of green-leaved and white-trunked aspen trees. One time, driving up to hike with Tim and a few friends, we saw a big-horned sheep on the side of a slope and deer were common up here, too.

Travis pulls off the road onto a small, steep, gravel road.

"Does she live out here by herself?" I ask. "It's so remote."

"Has to. In Denver, you can't have more than five cats. Out here, no one pays much attention."

We pull up to a wood cabin with a dark-green metal roof sitting in a clearing surrounded by towering trees. As we get close, I realize the place is *huge*. Floor to ceiling windows line the front of the house and balconies wrap around both floors, facing the city somewhere out on the plains behind us. A late model SUV and a newish electric car sit in the driveway.

"Wow. She lives alone here? How rich is this woman?" I ask.

"Rich. Her family owns half of Aspen."

I eye him. "You have very interesting patients."

He grins. "In more ways than one."

The front door opens, and a woman slips out, shutting the door quickly behind her. She's pretty, with glossy brown hair, a slim figure, and fashionable glasses—cat-eyed of course. And she's not very old, maybe late twenties. Much younger than I expected when Travis mentioned a cat lady.

She's wearing joggers and a T-shirt featuring a poster that says, *Wanted: Dead and Alive,* and under that, *Schrodinger's Cat.* I have no idea what it means, but the cat on the wanted poster is cute.

Travis waves at her through the windshield, then climbs through to the back to gather up some supplies from various drawers and the mini-fridge. Beatrix waits for us outside.

"Is she bringing the cats out here?" I ask.

"No, we'll go in for this one. It would take all day to load them in carriers and bring them out." He climbs out of the RV by the side door, opens my door, and helps me down.

"Hey, Bea," Travis says. "I'd like you to meet my friend, Amelia. She's riding along today. Is it okay if she comes in?"

The woman turns her eyes to me. One is a pretty, swirly color, like when aspen leaves are halfway between turning from green to yellow and brown in fall. The other is blue. Interesting. After a second, she nods.

"Come in quick. I don't want anyone to slip out."

If it was nighttime, I'd worry we were stepping in to one of those B-rated horror films where girls like me always end up tripping over their own feet, falling, and getting ax murdered. But as slight as Beatrix was, maybe the ax murderer would get her first. Wait, maybe she *is* the ax murderer. . . .

She slips inside, and Travis tips his head, inviting me to follow her.

"How many cats does she have, really?" I whisper.

He shakes his head. "To be honest, I'm not sure."

At first glance, a home with possibly ninety-nine cats doesn't look all that unusual. A two-story great room is tastefully decorated with a lot of polished wood and minimal stuff— a leather sectional, several expensive-looking chairs, and a solid stone coffee table. A huge, stone fireplace dominates one wall, a thick area rug covers the wood floor, and a couple of thirsty-looking plants sit under the windows.

The biggest sign of Beatrix's housemates isn't cat scratches or toys, but the *smell*. Cat pee is distinct. It seems to be coming from somewhere near the back of the house. How many litter boxes do ninety-nine cats need?

"How have you been, Bea?" Travis asks while looking around. His nose wrinkles a bit, and concern flits across his face.

She shrugs, her thin shoulders darting up and down quickly. "Okay, I guess. I'm working on a new series."

"Bea is an author." Travis smiles at her, and her mouth softens a bit in response.

"What do you write?" I ask, thinking she'll say science fiction. Her shirt has something to do with physics, I think.

"Romance novels."

My eyebrows shoot up. "Really? Like, the spicy kind?"

She shrugs. "All kinds. Steamy, sweet, paranormal, contemporary."

Travis and I nod like this makes complete sense. Only . . . looking around the place, there's no signs that other humans ever set foot in the place. Where does she get her . . . er, inspiration?

She doesn't say much else, as if she's not even used to *speaking* to humans.

"Are you ready to do this?" Travis asks her.

Beatrix walks into the kitchen, coming back out a moment later with a tray piled high with round tins of cat food and one black Sharpie marker. She sets the tray down on a long wood dining table supported by two massive pedestals. Eight chairs fit comfortably around the thing, although I see a layer of dust on their seats.

She picks up a single can. "Ready."

Travis pulls a handful of syringes out of his bag, uncaps a few, and lays them on the table. Then he nods to her without speaking, as if this is a ritual they have performed before. Bea squares her shoulders and cracks open the tin.

Movement suddenly erupts around me. Rocket launches of tails, paws, and whiskers in an astonishing combination of cat colors and patterns fire from every possible hiding place around the room. They shoot from under the couch, dart down the stairs, leap from behind curtains, and bolt from the kitchen, sprinting past me to gather around their mistress as if she held a live mouse instead of an ordinary tin of food.

As they arrive, Travis scoops the closest cat up with one hand —a beautiful golden tabby with stripes like a tiger—and plunges a syringe into the kitty's haunch. The cat howls and hisses as if Travis is pulling out its whiskers instead. He releases it, and Bea offers it the tin of food on the table. While it's eating, she marks the inside of its ear with the Sharpie. Ah, that's what the marker is for. Keeping track of who got jabbed.

At first, the other cats are more focused on the food than on what Travis is doing. He's able to stick five more in under a minute. He works as fast as he can, but the cats keep coming. They crowd around Bea, mewing and yowling like a sinister cat cloud.

Okay, he wasn't actually kidding about Bea's ninety-nine problems. There have to be at least that many in here. When Travis stops to dig in his bag for a fresh supply of syringes, I step into the fray.

"Can I help? I can pick them up and hold them. Then you'll have two hands to give them the shot."

Travis wipes his sweating forehead. "We'll try it. But the first time you're bitten, you're out. I don't want to get sued." He throws me a quick grin.

I've never owned a cat, but I've spent time with them at friends' homes. They're sweet and furry and fun to pet. But that's apparently when they *want* to be held. Holding a writhing handful of feline flesh that wants nothing more than to escape your grasp is something else altogether.

I grab the first one and check its ears. No mark, so I hold it for Travis. The second one bites me right off the bat, but I do my best not to react, and Travis is too busy to notice. He immunizes it, and I hand it to Beatrix, immediately grabbing for the next. For some reason, the howls of their friends don't stop the other cats from crowding around the food anyway. I grit my teeth and hang on for dear life.

Twenty stressful minutes, five scratches, and two bites later, we're finished. Or at least Travis ran out of syringes. After the last of the tins opens, the cats melt back into their hiding places, minus ten or twelve who seem comfortable enough now to wander around the kitchen and living room.

One in particular shadows Beatrix closely, a tiny, thin gray cat that mewls pitifully. She picks it up, and it nibbles playfully on her thumb.

Bea invites us into the very large, very clean kitchen to wash our hands. My hands and forearms tingle and burn from all the bites and scratches, but it was satisfying to have contributed.

"How do we know we got them all?" I ask.

Travis shakes his head. "We don't. Probably did miss a few. Bea will check their ears this week, and we'll get the ones we missed next visit."

She throws him an appreciative look. "I don't know what I'd do without Dr. Travis. I couldn't bring all of my babies in to a clinic. It would take all week."

Dr. Travis. Now that I think about it, his patients make him sound like a veterinarian tapped to provide pet advice on a popular talk show. Actually, if Ellen needed a pet expert, *Dr. Travis* would be a fantastic choice. He's handsome, charming, and smart. Female viewers would go bonkers for him.

"How did you get all your cats?" I ask Beatrix.

"I took my first ten or so in as fosters. Then I adopted ten or so more." Bea looks around, her expression bewildered. "Now I have so many, it seems pointless to turn them away. I don't go to the shelters anymore, at least. People bring strays to me."

"It's kind of you to rescue them," I say.

"I can't not do it." She kisses the head of the cat in her arms, and her face droops as if remembering something sad. Trust-fund baby or not, Beatrix looks like someone who's had her disappointments. Then again, who hasn't? I've had my fair share recently.

"What else can I do for you, Bea?" Travis asks.

"That's it for this time." She thanks us for our help.

"It was fun." And I mean it. A lot better than pushing emails around behind the cold reception desk at HHB.

Travis gathers his bag. "See you next time. Take care of yourself and your family."

I tell her good-bye, and we slip through the door again, watching for escapees.

As we climb back in the RV, I hit my bitten and scratched hand on the door and wince. Travis's eyebrows pull together.

"Your arms are all red. Were you bitten? Let me see that." I sit and hold them out to him. "Why didn't you tell me? Cat bites can be nasty. I should treat those."

We climb in the back again so he can apply antibacterial cream and a couple of bandages. When he finishes, he holds my hands gently with both of his. The crackle I felt last time we touched returns. His eyes meet mine. My heart skips a beat, but after a moment, he lets go.

Oddly disappointed, I settle in the passenger seat and buckle up as he starts the RV.

"What's up with Bea and all those cats?" I ask. "She seems pretty young to be a cat hoarder." I'd watched the show. Sometimes people didn't only collect stuff, they collected animals, too.

"I don't think that's her problem. She lost an important person once, and she hasn't really recovered. I think she collects cats to have an excuse not to get out in the world and get her heart broken again."

I know what that feels like. "Where to next?" I ask as he pulls the RV back onto the mountain road, heading downhill this time.

"West Denver. A patient has a gut blockage."

"That sounds serious. What kind of animal?"

"Boa constrictor."

My mouth drops open. "A . . . snake?"

"Yep. Nine-footer."

Nine feet? I twitch. "Will you need help with it?"

"Only if he gets himself around me."

"Give me Jo's number. If that happens, I'll notify next of kin."

The boa, Mr. Stricture, is having trouble digesting his last mouse meal. Travis recommends rubbing its belly to get the poor mouse moving, which I help with. I never thought I'd give a snake a massage, but there it is.

We check on a couple of labs with sweet, graying faces, milky eyes, and slow wagging tails, an irritable goose called Belle with some sort of hitch in her honk, and a few other assorted animals.

Finally, at around four in the afternoon, we're finished. We stop at a convenience store for cold drinks, then Travis points the Love & Pets RV toward downtown.

"You did a great job today," he says. "Have you ever thought about working with animals?"

I blink, surprised. "No."

"You should. You're good with them."

"Isn't vet school like three years long? And expensive?"

"You don't have to be a veterinarian, unless you want to. You could be a tech, like Jo. It takes less time, and the pay isn't bad."

I let that sink in. I do love animals, and the work seems interesting and varied. I liked biology, and I don't mind blood very much. But the thought of more school, and more tuition debt, makes me cringe.

"I don't know."

He sips his drink and puts it back in the cup holder. "While you're thinking about it . . . how about dinner? You earned it."

His voice is casual, and he keeps his eyes on the wheel, but the muscles in his arms tense.

A vision of Tim, his blond hair shining against my pillow, paints itself in my mind. I almost say no. Except—that movement in Tim's bed in Bali was no giant Indonesian spider.

I had a wonderful day with Travis. And better yet, he's here, beside me, asking me to spend more time with him. I touch his arm, and the muscles relax.

"I'd love to."

Chapter Fifteen

Travis drops me at home to shower and change. He'll do the same, then come back downtown in his car. As I walk Doug, my heart thumps in weird ways, and my whole body feels flushed, like I'm coming down with some kind of exotic snake flu.

After a shower and blow-dry, I put on a fitted strappy dress and heels. I fluff my hair, smooth on lipstick, and smile at myself in the dresser mirror to check my teeth. My cheeks are pinker than usual, and the shadows under my eyes have receded. Doug curls up on the bed, his back to me, as if he knows my plan.

Avery looks me up and down when I walk into the living room. "Uh, where are you going dressed like that?"

"Travis asked me to dinner."

Her eyes widen. "And you're going?"

I hold out my arms, letting my outfit speak for me.

She jumps off the couch and wraps me in a hug. "I'm *so* glad, Mel. You deserve this."

"It's only dinner."

She pulls away and nods knowingly. "That's what *you* think. Where are you going? Do you need a ride?"

"No, we're meeting at the Cactus."

"Maybe Jason and I will show up there for a drink. I'd like to see Travis Brewer, DVM, again."

"Please Avery, don't tease me. He's only thanking me for helping him do his rounds today."

"Sure. That's all it is."

"Avery, I'm warning you. I will slip Doug poop in your bed tonight if you show up."

She gags. "Anything but that." She hugs me again. "Have fun. Please. You haven't in so long."

I'm halfway to the restaurant before I realize I didn't say good-bye to Doug. How could I forget?

Travis is waiting out front when I arrive. He smiles when he sees me, and after a second, kisses me on the cheek. Flames burst in my gut.

He's wearing a deep-blue collared shirt, jeans, and nice leather boots. His hair is loose to his shoulders, and he has a sprinkling of sexy stubble. His smell is chocolate cake and wood smoke. Heavenly.

He takes my hand, and we step inside to the hostess. Every bit of my attention is on the feel of my skin against his.

The Blue Cactus is full but not packed. Still, I doubt we can get a table at their popular rooftop deck. Until Travis gives her his name.

"Did you make a reservation?" I ask.

He smiles, dazzling me as usual. "After I dropped you off to shower. I like to be prepared."

The server leads us upstairs to a table facing west to the foothills, and Travis pulls out my chair for me. The mountains look hazy but beautiful in the late afternoon sun. When our waiter comes, Travis orders a beer, and I get a local cider. I lean back in my chair and let the sun soak into my skin. I've missed this.

"Missed what?" he asks.

"What?" I bolt up.

His head cocks to the side. "You said you missed this."

"Oh. Did I?" I bury my face in the cider glass the waiter puts down.

"What do you miss?"

"Um, going out, I guess. I mean, I've been busy at work, and Doug's been such a handful . . ." My voice trails off.

Travis tips his beer, watching the foam float against the side, then looks back at me. He's not buying it, I can tell.

"I've . . . had a hard time. Since Tim left," I say.

"What's he doing in Indonesia? I don't think you've told me."

Hesitantly, I tell him about Global Ballers and Tim's goal to fund it.

Travis leans toward me, one hand on his beer, both eyes on me. He nods and asks questions. He isn't one of those people who listen only to find the next chance to talk themselves.

"Sounds like a great cause." His voice is sincere.

"The Love & Pets Party is amazing, too."

I wince. No one said Travis's event *wasn't* amazing. And this isn't a competition. I try again. "What you're doing for people and their pets right here in Denver is inspiring."

"Thanks. Jo always says you can do big things in small ways. That stuck in my head."

"I like it." I move the menu around, then ask something I've been wondering all day. "How's she doing?"

He gulps his beer and stares out at the street. "Not well. I know when an animal's dying. It's not that much of a stretch to know when a human is, too. I'm trying to prepare myself, but . . ." He shakes his head.

I reach for his hand. "I'm so sorry. She's a sweet lady. I'd love to know her better."

He keeps his eyes trained on the hills. "She likes you. She said you have a gentle spirit."

My eyes prickle. Gentle. Sometimes I feel like that's a derogatory word these days, like we're all supposed to be hard-driving and powerful all the time. But I'll take it.

Travis goes on. "She's one of a kind. She raised me, you know?

Mom liked the bottle. Sometimes pills, too. I didn't really know my father. So Jo took me in. She used to keep an eye on all the kids on the block, when their parents weren't around much—or weren't sober—and feed them, take care of them. And all her pets." He smiles, but it's weak. "I don't know how she managed it on one salary."

"Where's your Mom now?"

His eyes narrow. "She sobered up after being diagnosed with cirrhosis when I was a junior in high school, but she was pretty sick. She died from complications a year later." He blinks a little, his eyes bright. "Sorry. It still feels fresh sometimes."

He doesn't try to hide his emotions. He owns them. I love that.

Travis cares. Not only about the score of the last Broncos game, or the best place to rock climb or mountain bike, or his career. About people—and animals, of course. He's a good man. Something stirs inside me, a realization that I have something here. An opportunity. A rare gem hidden in plain sight.

The waitress arrives to take our order. I tell her what I'd like while Travis pulls himself together. He orders a burger; I get a quesadilla.

"Jo sounds like a saint," I say.

"Ha. Not exactly. When she still dated, she had a run of terrible boyfriends. And cigarettes were a crutch, of course. But she shielded me from most of her problems, and Mom's. And her steady stream of rescue animals gave me a start on my work. She took in kids, but she also took in any pet that people couldn't care for anymore. She had everything from puppies to a juvenile gator."

I almost spit out my cider. "An alligator?"

"Yep. Someone got Lola as a baby, but by age two, she'd outgrown her cage. Could barely turn around in that thing. Jo found her a home at the gator rescue out near Alamosa. Have you been there?"

I shake my head.

"It's wild—out on the high plains in the mountains, where you should see antelope or coyote, but instead there are all these reptiles from alligators to iguanas to snakes. A lot of them started out as pets, but when they grew too big or too dangerous, the rescue took them in."

"How do they survive in the winter?" Temperatures can be below freezing up there.

"Geothermal water. They love it. Like nice, warm baths."

I shake my head. "Sounds . . . out there."

"I was mesmerized the first time I saw the place. Jo and I took Lola there ourselves when I was about ten."

"How did you get her there?" I pictured Jo driving through the mountains, an alligator hanging out in the back seat.

"She borrowed a small trailer to hitch behind her truck and took her in her cage. I've been back once or twice. They do good work."

"So do you."

"Thanks, Amelia. That means a lot." His smile makes me want to think of more compliments. "I've talked enough, though. Tell me more about your job and family."

I groan. "No thanks. I don't want to put you to sleep. My life's not all that interesting compared to yours."

"C'mon. Sure it is. What's it like working at a law office?"

I tell him a few stories about HHB. Like how Jim has this horrible habit of digging in his ears then nibbling his nails in meetings, and Cassie finds subtle ways to flirt with Max. Then I tell him about Forty, and how he once fell asleep during a client meeting, and Kenny, who I don't think I can survive without. Travis laughs —a real laugh, not just polite—his eyes crinkling adorably each time.

I tell him about my parents, how Mom worked all the time to support us after Dad moved to Cincinnati with his new wife. How I've always leaned on Avery for support. I *don't* tell him how I wish I didn't have to keep turning to her when things go wrong in my life, like when Tim left and I had to move back in with her. I'm not ready to talk about Tim.

We lean closer as we talk and eat, and the clinking of glasses, the laughter of other diners, and the cars driving by down below fade. I'm only aware of Travis's smiles, his thoughtful questions, the hints of sadness in his eyes.

I study his lips as he speaks, thin but soft. I could kiss him. I *want* to kiss him. The surprise of that realization pushes me back in my chair. I haven't wanted to kiss anyone but Tim in a long, long time. Not even Max, as fabulous as he seemed at first.

Time stops while I process the feeling, so I'm not even sure what Travis is saying when a woman's voice breaks through my thoughts.

"Trav? What are you doing downtown?"

Chapter Sixteen

A woman stands beside our table. She's about my age, with a mane of shiny black hair and flawless skin. She's wearing a tiny tank top, showing off her abs, and a denim miniskirt that flatters her long legs. Sparkly earrings hang from her ears, and her fingertips are painted a glossy black. She's *gorgeous*.

Travis blinks twice, as if he just woke up. "Tania. How are you?"

"I'm great. Yeah."

He stares at her for a second, like he's dazed, then seems to remember me. "This is my friend, Amelia. Amelia, this is my . . . Tania."

My Tania? I throw him a puzzled glance but shake her hand and say hello. My own fingernails are chipping, I notice.

Tania's eyebrows pull together, although she continues to smile at Travis. "I thought you hated coming downtown."

He waves a hand. "Oh, well, Amelia lives nearby."

"City girl, huh?" She studies me. There's no hostility or cattiness in her words.

I nod and smile politely. I didn't know Travis hated downtown. We didn't have to come here.

She turns back to him. "It's been a while. How have you been? How's Jo?" From her tone, I can tell she knows Jo's ill.

"She's hanging in there. You know her; she's not going to complain. How's your family? And—Dante?"

Travis's eyes shoot left and right, like he wishes he could escape the conversation. He taps a spoon on the metal table and moves around in his seat. I've never seen him look so jumpy. In fact, I realize one of the things I appreciate about him is how unflappable he always seems, even when a pug knocks him on his butt, he's working alongside a woman in a dog costume, or when he's facing the terminal illness of someone he loves.

Who is this woman with the power to shake him up?

"They're good. Mama and Poppi ask about you and Jo. They'd love to see you."

"Yeah, that would be great." His words sound forced.

"Um, how do you know each other?" I ask.

They share a look. I can't read everything that flows between them in those milliseconds, but if Tim walked in right now, I'd bet we'd have a similar look.

Tania glances to her left. "Here's D now."

A handsome dark-haired guy moves across the deck toward us. His chestnut skin and black, wavy hair are set off by a tight white shirt. She takes his arm.

"Dante." Travis stands and shakes the guy's hand. Travis' body is stiff, but he looks determined to be polite. As they pump hands, both of their arm muscles tense.

The guy holds up a coaster with a glowing red circle in the center. "Our table's ready, babe. Nice to see you, man."

Tania smiles at me again with genuine friendliness. And in a swirl of hair and flowery perfume, she's gone.

Travis swigs his beer.

"Are you okay?" I ask.

"Yeah. Sorry. I should have known I might run into her. The restaurant name rang a bell when you suggested it earlier, but I couldn't remember why. Now I remember T came here with her girlfriends all the time."

T? The familiarity makes my chest ache. A hot, itchy feeling creeps over my shoulders and across my chest. Is it . . . jealousy? Ridiculous. Travis and I have known each other for like two seconds. We aren't even dating. But I can't stop myself from asking.

"So, she's your . . . ?"

"Tania was my fiancé." He looks a little pale.

Fiancé. I almost forgot he said he was engaged once. I'm not sure I want to know the details of how long they were together, or what broke them up, and he definitely doesn't seem excited to tell me about it.

I gesture at our ravaged plates. "Do you want to go? Maybe walk down by the creek?"

"Yeah, sure."

His shoulders pull back. I get out my wallet to help pay the tab, but distractedly he throws some bills down on the table, pulls out my chair, and we squeeze ourselves through the crowded patio.

It's a relief to escape the press of buildings on either side as we reach the Cherry Creek walking path. The sun is setting, making me wish I had my light sweater. Colorado cools off quickly in the evening, even in summer. I move a little closer to his warm body, and he takes my hand. It feels natural.

"I'm sorry about how I acted. I haven't run into Tania like that since we broke off our engagement last year. I thought I was ready, but it was harder than I thought it would be." He rolls his neck, like a weight hangs from it.

I've never been engaged, but I understand. I miss Tim. Texting with him during the day. Snuggling with him at night. His antics with Doug. Hanging out with friends together. How would it feel to see him now, after he's been gone so long?

As I walk beside another, very different type of man, one I'm beginning to have feelings for, I wonder: Do I miss having Tim? Or do I just miss having *someone*?

When we reach the bridge over to the giant REI flagship store, we take a seat on the rocks beside the creek. Kids wade in the water, splashing each other, their shirts and shorts soaked. They squeal with happiness.

After a minute, I feel Travis shift toward me. I look over, and he's watching me. His hand slides up my arm, slowly, gently. He leans in close, his eyes on my chin, my cheeks, my eyebrows and forehead, my eyes. And finally, my lips. His soft breath warms my mouth.

Then he waits, waits to see if I'll move away, look down, or maybe push him off the rock. But I don't do any of those things, of course. Instead, our lips meet.

His are firm and taste of hoppy beer. They move slowly against mine at first, then his breath hitches, and he presses closer. His hands close on either side of my neck and slide under my hair. His tongue touches mine, just a little, asking. I accept, and the kiss suddenly sends a hot flush down my back and between my breasts. I gasp a little and move closer, my hand on his waist.

After minutes, hours, days, we pull back. He caresses my shoulder, his eyes roaming my face. A pulse in his neck beats frantically. My body feels elastic, like every cell suddenly loosened up.

"Amelia." Travis says my name softly. His hand moves to my hip. "Do you want to go . . ."

Home with him? Does he think after one admittedly hot kiss, I'd run to his bed with him?

Um, yes, my body says, but a part of my brain, however small, pulls back. I'm not sure I'm ready for that.

". . . to Pug Paradise again this week?"

"Oh!" I sit up straight. "Um, sure."

"I thought you might want to bring Doug to see the other pugs again."

"Definitely."

I lean against him and close my eyes, savoring the memory of our kiss. I'll see Travis again soon. I can't think of anything I want more. Except—*maybe*—Tim showing up at my door begging me to come back.

Chapter Seventeen

Brenda isn't available over the weekend. She's heading to Iowa to pick up a few new rescues. But she invites us out to Pug Paradise on Friday evening. I sneak out of work a little early, and Doug and I grab a Lyft out to Travis's house. Muzzle on, of course. Jo is coming with us, and I don't want them to have to come all the way downtown to get us.

Jo waits outside on the front porch, one hand shielding her face from the sun. I'm pretty sure she quickly stubs out a cigarette as Travis opens the door carrying her oxygen tank. From the stiffening of his body, I think he sees it, too.

He helps her down the steps. Doug and I climb out of the back seat. A smile warms Jo's face when I reach to give her a hug. I can barely feel any pressure in her frail embrace. I offer her the front seat of Travis's SUV, which she takes.

She leans on him as she gets in, and he buckles her seatbelt for her, like a child. He moves slowly, touching her so gently I want to cry. Her smile of thanks is weary.

I hop in the back with Doug, keeping him muzzled and leashed, just in case. He's using every last one of his wrinkles to scowl at Travis behind the wheel.

"I heard you had quite the day last weekend," Jo says to me as we get on the road.

"We did. It was amazing. I can't remember the last time I had such a blast."

"Now, who all did you see?"

I run down the various animals Travis treated, including Mr. Stricture and his serpent massage.

She laughs. "You did get the whole banana, didn't you?"

"Peel and all." Travis responds without missing a beat, as if it's something they say often.

Doug gives a wheezy sigh, makes two neat circles, and settles beside me, nose to back toes.

"And you met poor Bea." Jo shakes her head. "I worry about that girl. She's too young to live the way she does."

Travis lifts an eyebrow at me in the rearview mirror. "Jo worries about all my patients . . . and their animals, too. Amelia helped with the vaccinations at Bea's place and got a few bites for her trouble."

"Travis," Jo clucks her tongue. "You made her help with all those cats with no training?"

I lean forward. "I wanted to. We had an assembly line going, with Bea opening cans of food, me snatching up the cats, and Travis jabbing them. Honestly, I didn't blame them for turning on me a few times."

Jo nods. "Bea has more cats than sense. But she loves her animals, and anyone who does is a friend of mine." Wistfulness passes over her face. "I guess I won't see her again."

Travis slams a fist on the top of the steering wheel, making me jump. "Jo, don't talk like that."

"I know you don't like to hear the truth, love, but you have to face it, sooner or later."

He grips the wheel as if he might tear it from the steering column. His jaw clenches and a muscle over his right eye twitches. I touch his shoulder.

His grandmother's smile is sad. "My boy has never liked to talk about things he can't fix. Not that he can't handle them—Lord knows he's had to whether he likes it or not. But I think that's why he went into veterinary medicine. He never could stand to see an animal in pain, or a person for that matter."

He stares straight ahead at the highway. I don't know what to say, so I just listen.

"His patients are lucky. He's a fine veterinarian and a fine man. Anyone who spends even a little time with him can see that."

"I know." My voice is small, barely louder than the engine and road noise.

Travis gives me a long, searching look in the mirror. Heat boils from that look, singeing my skin. But he speaks to Jo.

"I wouldn't be anything without you, Jo-Jo. You know that."

"I set your feet on the path, love. You climbed the mountain yourself."

She settles back against the seat and puts her oxygen tubing in her nose, as if all the talking has exhausted her.

The rest of the ride out to Pug Paradise is quiet, but not awkward. Jo's words spread a blanket over us. Not a cozy, comfortable one, but one that pulled us together anyway.

Brenda waits for us outside, and again she's in her pug onesie. Travis opens the passenger door and helps Jo out and over to the fenced enclosure. Doug starts to whine as soon as he hears the other dogs barking. I open the back door, and he drags me to the fence.

Ignoring Travis, for once, he's completely focused on the pugs. His tail is erect, his body tense.

"Well. Looks like Douglas might be ready to meet the puglets today," Brenda's voice booms.

There are five inside the enclosure this time. Two pugs, new ones I think, play tug of war with a piece of rope while another chases its tail until it suddenly flops over. The big guy is still here. He lies on the ground in the shade, panting and scratching inside a flopped-over ear. The fifth, Daisy, is focused right back on Doug.

She stands on the other side of the fence, just out of his reach, and barks sharply.

Doug looks entranced.

Brenda raises an eyebrow. "You want to meet her this time, Romeo?"

I clutch his leash. I know this is why we're here, but I'm nervous. "I don't know. What if he fights with them?"

"We'll take it slow. Keep the muzzle on at first." She reaches for Doug's leash. "Sometimes you have to unstick your feet from the ground to face your fears. Doug looks ready to face his. How about you?"

I breathe deeply. Right. This isn't about me, it's for Doug. I hand her the leash, and she leads him to the gate. I move to stand next to Jo and Travis at the fence.

As Doug goes in, the tail chaser prances over. The two playing tug-of-war drop the rope and sniff around Brenda's scuffed boots. The big guy stays where he is, although he stops scratching to watch. Daisy marches closer, her eyes on Doug.

Doug goes still—the kind of still that usually means he's about to lose it on someone. When I bite my lip and grip the fence, Jo places a comforting hand on my arm.

The pugs are inches away now. My breath quickens.

Without warning, Doug yanks the leash out of Brenda's hands and tears in circles around the pen. His ears slap up and down as he runs, his tail curls tightly over his back, and his backside tucks under, as if he worries someone might take a bite.

The puglets bark as they give chase, making an incredible racket. The big guy doesn't bother to join, but he watches, head up, and adds his deeper woof to the din.

At first, I think Doug might stop by me, begging me to get him out of this hellhole. I call to him just in case he forgot where I am, but he ignores me. After he passes me for the third time, three pugs tumbling after him, I realize he doesn't want to escape. He's having fun.

Each dog tries to run him down and each misses. All except for Daisy.

She watches as Doug races around the pen, then after about three rounds, pounces on his leash. He drops and rolls. I cringe, expecting him to snarl and go for her throat. Instead, he leaps to his feet and chases her in the opposite direction. The other pugs join in.

He tumbles his new friend. She gets to her feet and leaps on him, followed by the others, creating a pug pile.

The pugs rush one way, then the other. And after a few minutes, they collapse near the big guy, in the shade, breathing hard, pink tongues lolling and droopy faces upturned in distinctly doggy grins. Doug pants hardest and happiest of all.

Brenda takes the muzzle off, so Doug can drink some water. He and Daisy lie near each other for a few minutes, and then, as if a silent gunshot goes off, they start racing around again.

Brenda and Jo get to chatting, and Travis takes my hand, leading me away from them.

"Amelia, I wanted to tell you again I'm sorry about how I acted around Tania. If you don't mind, I'd like to explain."

Mind? I was dying of curiosity about her and what happened between them. But I just nod.

"Tania and I grew up in the same neighborhood." He glances at his grandmother. "Jo used to take care of her once in a while when her parents took off. We relied on each other, you know?"

I nod. Avery and I did, too. Especially when Mom was going through one of her moods.

"We dated in high school and then went to Metro together. She came with me to Fort Collins when I went to vet school." He puts a hand on the fence and keeps his eyes on the pugs as he talks. "Tania worked the whole time I was in school. She was supportive, although I knew she got tired of it. She always talked about me joining a lucrative vet practice when I graduated, maybe even starting my own in a few years." His smile thinned. "She wasn't counting on a used RV and a ranchette full of rejected animals in the suburbs."

Jo coughs. He turns toward her, ready to help. When she stops, he goes on.

"Anyway, after a while, she started to pull away." His face twists a little, but the smile never really comes through. "She started hiding her phone from me, erasing texts, but one day she left it out, and I saw a text message on her phone from someone called *D*. And they weren't talking about the weather."

Tim's moving bedsheets come to mind.

He shrugs. "She moved out a couple weeks later. Dante owns his own construction company, and I guess he does really well. I don't know. I didn't realize it at the time, but I think we wanted different things. We grew up pretty poor, and she always said she never wanted to be poor again. I would have given her anything; I just thought she'd be willing to wait for it a little longer."

"I'm sorry, Travis. You didn't deserve that."

He shrugs and watches the older women talk. "I wish she'd just told me what she wanted instead of sneaking around, lying to me. After growing up together, that hurt more than that she didn't want a life together. Anyway, I wanted you to know what happened. After Tania, I don't want any more secrets and lies."

I put my hand on his. I understand.

A few minutes later, Brenda clips Doug's leash back on and leads him out to me with no muzzle. He trots out like he owns the place.

I scoop him up and bury my face in the wrinkles on his head. He smells like dog spit, but I don't care. He's happy, and for the first time in a long time, *I'm* happy.

I thank everyone in turn, saving my brightest smile for Travis. His expression turns my bones to jelly. I don't know why he looks at me like that, since I'm covered in pug fur and shiny from the sun. But I feel fantastic.

"Will you bring Douglas back next week?" Brenda asks as we load ourselves into the SUV.

Travis and I answer *yes* at the same time. His voice is low and scratchy; mine is too high. Jo and Brenda exchange a look, then a hug.

"Good to see you, Jo," Brenda says gently. "You take care of yourself."

"I will. If I don't, my grandson gets very upset."

Before he gets in the car, Doug stares back at the pen, where the other pugs are resting. He whines, eyes focused on one of them in particular. Daisy stands at the fence. Then he sleeps all the way back to Denver.

I muzzle him before we hop out on the curb at my apartment, and I speak to Jo through her window. "I'm coming over soon to help Travis finalize plans for the party. Will you be there?"

"No plans to be anywhere else, love," she says.

Love. What she calls Travis. Her light brown eyes, so similar in shape to his, look content. I kiss her cheek.

Travis walks Doug and me to the door, but before we arrive, he pulls me into his arms.

People walk by, and I catch a glimpse of a neighbor staring as they go inside, but we don't hesitate. Our lips find each other as if they were long-separated mates. His hands slide around to my neck and back, pulling me against him.

When his tongue touches my lips, I open my mouth and gently push him against the wall. Heat floods my body, and sweat rushes to my skin. My breath comes fast. He tastes sweeter than any sugary candy, and his body is hard in all the right places. I twine my fingers in his hair and kiss him deeper.

Dimly, I wonder if Jo is watching, what she might be thinking. At the moment, I don't care. I couldn't stop kissing Travis if I tried.

We only break apart when a police siren blares five feet away, its blue-and-red lights bouncing off the glass and chrome of the apartment building. A cop car sits behind Travis's car, and a few seconds later, a bald officer gets out.

"You making a delivery? Because if not, you've got to move this vehicle."

Travis kisses me once more, gently, his hands on my hips. Fourth of July colors shoot through me, and I lean into him. When we threaten to dive into another kiss, the officer clears his throat.

"*Now*, sir."

Travis pulls back, eyes on me. "I'll call you tomorrow."

With an apology and an ear-to-ear grin for the officer, he hurries around the SUV to the driver's side and carefully pulls into traffic. I wave. Shaking his head, the officer gets back in his car.

Leash in hand, I float through the lobby. Manuel greets me with one eyebrow raised.

"Have a nice day?"

"I had a *great* day, Manuel. How was yours?"

He shrugs. "*Bueno*. But the best part about it is in *cinco minutos*."

"What happens then?" My voice sounds dreamy, and my thoughts are still a little muddled.

"I go home."

I finally wake up a little. "Crap! Is it really almost eight o'clock?"

"*Sí.*" He looks puzzled.

The sun stays up so long in summer. I hadn't noticed how late it was.

"Did you forget to do something?" he asks.

I take a deep breath, composing myself. "I did. But you know what? It's okay. I'm okay. You have a wonderful weekend, Manuel."

He gives me a funny look but nods and heads for his office while I turn to the elevator.

A few weeks ago, I would have rushed upstairs to my computer, full of apologies and excuses, afraid that I screwed things up. Not today. I'm not going to let a missed call ruin what was one of the best days of the last six months.

Tim can wait.

Chapter Eighteen

It takes willpower, but I don't call Tim back that night. I don't even call him back the next night.

I'm not trying to punish or torture him. I'm . . . testing my strength. And the weekend is busy. Saturday I go hiking with Avery and Jason and a couple of friends, and Travis, Jo, and I have a planning session on Sunday.

By Monday, I'm feeling good. I hum as I create invoices for last week's clients. Kenny actually stops working and leans back in his chair to look at me.

"What's up, Princess? You're in a good mood. Don't you know this is my last week?"

I groan. "Please don't remind me."

"Why so happy, then?"

I whisper-tell him about my semi-dates with Travis, how well Doug is doing, and that I've gone *seventy-two hours* without returning Tim's call.

He pats my hand. "Excellent job. Keep him guessing."

"No, I'm not trying to—"

But he's already moving on. "Does that vet of yours go to Park Hill? Chi-Chi needs his shots, and after Stinkers, Mama's afraid to take him out around other dogs that might give him something."

Kenny's mother got a new chihuahua last week. "I think so. Want me to ask?" I'm already reaching for my phone to call Travis. Any excuse to talk to him is a good one.

"Yes, please. If he does, I'll let Mama know she can make the appointment."

Max comes out of his office down the hall. He avoids eye contact as he passes us on the way to the restroom.

"Maybe I should just text him," I say in a low voice. Kenny goes back to typing.

Max still hasn't told me if he's planning to call animal control on Doug. Enough time has gone by that I'm starting to relax, but I try not to do anything that might make him change his mind.

By Tuesday night, Tim has called three times. I don't remember the last time that happened. Actually, I don't think it's *ever* happened. Doug and I were always right there by the computer every Friday night, waiting.

When the Skype call comes in that night, I'm in bed, texting with Travis. Doug is lying on his back, twitching as he chases a rabbit, or maybe his new friend Daisy. But the familiar ringtone jolts him awake. His mad scramble through the bedding to get to his feet, then onto the floor, is comical. I'm laughing as I answer the call.

"Amelia, where have you been? Is everything okay with Doug?" Tim's expression is more annoyed than worried.

I scoop up Doug and put him on my lap. He barks and whines at the sight of Tim, as usual, his curly tail whipping so hard that I have to lean back to keep from getting smacked.

"Sorry about that. I was busy Friday . . . and the last few days. But we're good, aren't we, Dougie?" I rub his sides and his stiff hair pokes me like little spears.

"Busy?" Tim's eyebrow pushes up. "With what?"

He's in his room, and in the full light of day on his side, it's clear his bed is empty this time. He's blonder and tanner than a week ago, if that's possible. He's glowing like some kind of sun god.

But . . . it doesn't take my breath away. In fact, I only feel mildly happy to see him. Part of my mind is back on the flirting I was doing with Travis before Tim called.

"Doug and I went out to the Pug Paradise rescue again. And Tim, he had *such* a breakthrough. He didn't bark or growl or freak out or anything. He just played with the other pugs like they were his best friends. It was so fantastic. I wish you could've seen him."

He runs a hand through his hair and shifts in his seat. Doug squirms in my arms, trying to jump on the keyboard.

"Did Avery take you?" Tim asks.

"No, Trav—Doctor Brewer did. The vet. Remember I told you about him?" I speak quicker. "Anyway, we had so much fun, didn't we, love?"

I say the last to Doug, realizing a second later that I used Jo's pet word for Travis.

Tim blinks, like something's confusing him. "Okay. That's good to hear. I'm glad you had a good day, Mel."

He hasn't called me Mel since he left. No one has, except Avery. His eyes stay on me longer than usual.

"And how are you, Lil' Dougie? Are you good?"

Doug lets out a sharp yip. I lift him up a bit so his nails can't dig so hard into my legs. If it wasn't for my pajama pants, I'd be punctured right now.

"I've missed you, buddy. I was worried something happened to you when you guys didn't answer at our usual time Friday night." Tim keeps looking at Doug. "Maybe next time you can let me know everything's okay if you aren't there when I call."

I roll my eyes. "Doug's a dog, Tim. He can't let you know anything. But if you ask *me* to, I will."

Emotions war on Tim's face. I see something like irritation first, then worry, and finally, suspicion. He clears his throat and adjusts something on his desk. "Are you upset with me, Amelia? Did I do something?"

I think about that. Did he? He left our relationship and home with almost no warning to move halfway around the world, breaking up with me in the process, and assuming I could find a place to live with his dog on a moment's notice. But he was honest at every step about what he wanted and where I stood.

So, did he do something wrong?

"No, Tim. Not really. I think I made the mistake."

"What was it?"

I smile. "Nothing. At least, nothing worth talking about now." I crane my neck to see Doug's face. "Hey Lil' Dougie, want to hear your favorite song?" I turn back to the screen. "Go ahead, Tim. Play it."

His lips thin and eyes scrunch, like he doesn't like how this conversation is going at all, but he pushes something on his computer, and "Girl, I Love You So Bad" starts to play. As usual, Doug maneuvers himself as close to Tim as he can, barking and wagging. He presses his nose into the screen, leaving a snotty streak.

But what has always seemed like such a sweet and endearing reaction to the song Tim taught him to love, the song he associates completely with Tim, now seems sort of . . . sad. Why do we do this to him? Why keep him stuck in the hope that he'll see Tim any day now, when he shows no sign of it? Why torment him?

Tim hasn't once committed to coming back on a particular date. In fact, he keeps putting me off when I ask. To Doug, this time he's been away must seem like an eternity.

Watching him, I speak over the music. "You know, Tim, I'm sorry, but I don't think this is a good idea anymore."

He turns the volume down. "What?"

I wave my hand at Doug, the computer, and him. "All of this. I'm not sure it's healthy for Doug, or for me, waiting for your call once a week, listening to that song." I rub my cheek, diving deep into my courage. "It's been hard since you left, Tim. For Doug and for me. We're just starting to kinda heal. So . . . maybe we shouldn't talk for a while."

Tim's eyes open wide, the sapphire blue flashing like sunlight off the Java Sea. Not that I know what that looks like personally, but I'd Google-stalked Tim's entrepreneur camp enough times to have an educated guess.

"Amelia, wait. I know you've been feeling—"

"No, Tim, I don't think you do know how I've felt. Not for a long time."

His jaw clenches before he speaks. "Maybe you're right, but you can't shut me out. I should at least be able to see Doug when I want to. He's my dog."

"Not really. You left him with me. I've tried to do what's best for him, and that's what I'm doing now. I think it's best for us both not to speak with you for a while."

"But, Amelia . . ."

"Good night, Tim. I'll let you know when we're ready to talk again." With a shaking finger, I disconnect.

And immediately burst into tears. The really ugly kind. I fall on my bed, face down in my pillow. Doug jumps up and sits beside me, licking my hand and whining.

I'm not even sure why I'm losing it. What I said to Tim feels right. I *have* been caring for Doug the best way I can, and I've been trying to get over Tim leaving. I don't know if it was seeing Doug happy at Pug Paradise that made me realize things were finally getting better for us or if missing Tim's call did the trick.

I only know I need space from him. And if I need space from him, then . . . do I love him anymore?

Out of nowhere, I feel Travis's hands wandering across my back and down to my hips. His lips on my skin. I see his smile that seems meant only for me. His kindness toward Jo and care for his patients and their owners.

Guilt pools in my stomach. Am I this fickle? A month ago, Tim was all I thought about. Even Max didn't move the needle. But spending time with Travis feels like more than a casual flirtation. His kisses promise something more. And I want to find out what it is.

My bed dips and squeaks as Avery sits beside me to rub my back. Her voice is soft when she speaks. "Want to talk about it?"

I open an eye. Doug's droopy face is right in front of me. If my nose wasn't still buried in the pillow, I'm sure I'd be getting a nostril full of dog breath. His tail wags tentatively. I scratch his neck.

"Tim and I broke up."

Avery hesitates. "Um . . . yeah. Didn't that happen months ago, Melly?"

A half-sob, half-hiccup rips out of me. Like I said—ugly tears. "Yes, but I think I finally got the message today. I told him not to call for a while."

Avery's hand doesn't stop its soothing circle, but I hear something that sounds like a soft *hallelujah*.

I go on. "It hurts too much to talk to him. Tonight, I realized that every time I did, it reminded me I wasn't good enough. That he didn't love me enough to stay together while he was gone. And I think talking to Tim, and that stupid song, hurts Doug, too." Doug lies down, eye to eye with me. "He had such a great weekend, Aves. I wish you'd seen him with those other pugs. I think he's ready to move on. Maybe we both are."

She squeezes my shoulder. "So how did you leave it with Tim?"

"That was it. I told him not to call."

"And what will you do now?"

"I don't know. Wait and see how this feels, I guess."

Avery pulls a tissue out of the box on my bedside table and gently wipes my face. "Well, this doesn't seem like a good start."

I pull myself back up to sitting. Doug burrows into my lap and rolls over for a tummy rub.

Avery hands me the tissue and sits back. "Are you okay?"

I wipe my nose and nod. "It was really hard to say those words to him, but I feel better now."

She smiles and smooths my hair. "Good. But . . . if you have to say them again, do me a favor? *Please* let me be there." Her eyes narrow evilly. "I want to see his face."

Chapter Nineteen

Tim doesn't call, not that I was expecting him to. Well, maybe a little. But he doesn't.

I spend the rest of the week mourning the loss of Kenny, even though he's not actually gone yet. Then Friday comes—the day I've been dreading—his last day.

"Kenny," I try not to whine as we walk back to work after an expensive lunch in his honor at a bistro several blocks away from the office. Jim, Cassie, and Max walk ahead, Forty shuffling a few steps behind them. "What will I do without you?"

He shakes his head and jokes, "That's what every man I've loved and left has said. You'll be fine, Princess. You survived Tim leaving, right?"

He's right. I was a hot mess, but I did survive. Only, this is *Kenny*. The man I spend at least eight hours a day with unless I manage to sneak out early; my work husband. How long will I make it at HHB without him? Jim was surprisingly sweet when he toasted Kenny at lunch, calling him his right-hand man. I think the partners will honestly miss him. But not as much as me.

"What are your plans for next week before classes start? And if you say study, I'm going to smack you. You have to do something fun."

He pushes his sunglasses up his nose and gives me a look. "I'll have you know that Ruston and I booked a last minute trip to PV."

"You did? That's fantastic!" Puerto Vallarta is one of their favorite spots. "How long are you going for?"

"Four days. This is low season, so we got an amazing deal at a little boutique hotel some friends recommended. We leave tomorrow."

"So romantic." I sigh, picturing them there walking on a pristine stretch of beach next to an azure sea, lying by the pool under swaying palm trees, having intimate dinners on a quiet terrace. When I see *myself* there, I jolt. It's not Tim smiling at me across the table with a glass of wine. It's Travis.

Kenny nudges me. "What?"

"Nothing, just imagining what a fabulous week you'll have." I hook my arm in his. "Kenny, in all seriousness, I will miss you so much. You've made working at HHB bearable. Thank you for being my friend."

He stops us and kisses the top of my head. "And I always will be. You'll be fine, Princess. More than fine. You've got a good heart."

A compliment from Kenny is like a rare sip of old, expensive wine. I squeeze his hand and savor it. "Thank you. We'll keep in touch, right?"

"Of course we will." We start walking again. "By the way, Travis saw Chi-Chi today. Mama texted and said he's a nice young man." He says the last three words in the slow voice he uses when he's imitating his mother.

"She did? Oh, I'm so glad she liked him. I can't wait for you to meet him. Hey! Maybe you and Ruston can come to the Love & Pets Party! It's going to be so much fun."

"Amelia, we don't have a pet."

"Well, come for the food. I got the Benny's Bodacious Bowls and Bovine Divine trucks to come."

Kenny makes a face.

"They'll have balloon animals . . ."

He opens the door for me to head into our building. "Oh, in *that* case, we'll be there. Can we get our faces painted, too?"

"Yes!"

I laugh, but my smile fades as he packs the last of his things. The partners come out to shake his hand, I give him a hug, and he's gone. My chest aches as I sit down to face the last few hours of work alone.

As I'm packing up to leave, I find an email from Max. The coward sent it just after he left for the day, probably so he wouldn't have to see me. He's reporting Doug to animal control.

My body twitches with nervous energy as I load a muzzled Doug into the back of a Lyft heading for Travis's home. He thought we could try introducing Doug to the Four Horsemen. Now, it seems more important than ever that we prove he can be socialized.

I told Avery about the email when I got home and forwarded it to Kenny, but I haven't responded to Max. What can I say? Nothing he'll tell animal control about Doug is untrue. I have to rely on Travis and maybe Brenda to help me convince the city that he doesn't need to be put down.

Some Lyft drivers could talk sweat out of an iceberg, but this one is the silent type. That's okay with me. I chew my lip and scratch Doug distractedly, trying to think of anything else to do.

I ask the driver to let me off at the end of Travis's driveway and give him an extra-big tip for letting Doug hitch a ride. The sun is setting behind the house, casting long shadows across the lawn.

Doug stops to sniff behind a pine tree at the edge of the driveway. I try to pull him along, but he's not having it. Clearly something fascinating occurred there, requiring a thorough investigation. As I wait, Travis's door opens. I raise a hand and open my mouth to call out, but the words dribble away.

Tania, her dark hair shining in the last of the sunlight, walks out. She's wearing a dress that shows every perfect curve, and a pair of rocking heels. Travis follows her.

She turns at the edge of the porch, says something to him. He responds. Then, she puts her hands on his shoulders and kisses him.

It's not a long kiss, but it's on the lips. Travis doesn't move or react. He doesn't pull away. He just stands there, his lips against hers. The same lips that were against mine less than a week ago.

Anger and humiliation burn from my scalp to my toes. I could see that Travis had unfinished business with his ex when I met her. Who doesn't? But I don't think that business should include kissing her when he's also kissing me.

I need to get out of here. Now.

My hands are shaking so bad, I can barely hold my phone still to open the Lyft app. As I juggle my phone and the end of the leash, Doug catches sight of the Horsemen careening down the porch steps. He runs at them, barking feverishly. The end of the leash jerks my hand, and my phone goes flying.

The other dogs race toward us, baying. Travis and Tania whirl my way, and with a sick twist of my gut, I step out from behind the tree to face them. Not knowing what else to do, I reel Doug in, lift him out of the dogs' reach, and give a weak wave.

When Travis calls the Horsemen back, they stop instantly, although they continue to bark. Tania gets in her car—a little black sedan that I hadn't noticed before. It's as sexy as she is. I stand to the side, still holding Doug, as she drives past.

Unbelievably, she smiles at me. Not a snotty, *He's still mine and there's nothing you can do about it* smile, just a normal, friendly one, but still. I do my best to return it, only my expression feels more like a grimace.

Travis jogs to his dogs, telling them to stay, which they do, and he walks over to me. Doug growls, his eyes locked on Travis.

"Amelia, I didn't know you were here." His expression is strange. Not guilty, but not happy to see me either. He looks . . . sad. "I'm sorry, I forgot to call you to cancel. I can't meet tonight."

My gut sinks about six inches. He and Tania are back together. It's the only answer. He saw her the other day, and she saw him. They realized they never should have broken up.

I shift Doug's weight into my left arm. "That's okay. I'll just call for a ride home."

My thumb reaches for the app, misses, and touches Spotify instead. A popular new song blares out until I can get it to stop. Sweat beads up along my forehead and under my arms, and I'm sure my face is an attractive shade of cotton-candy pink.

He holds up his hands. "Hang on, let me explain. Jo . . . she had to go into intensive care today. I need to leave right now to be with her. I just came home to feed the animals. I'm sorry, it all happened so fast I forgot to call you. She had an appointment with her oncologist today, and her oxygen levels were so low. They admitted her, and after a long talk with her doctors, they . . . called hospice in."

His voice breaks on the last words. I touch his arm, and Doug growls.

"Oh, Travis. I'm so sorry. What can I do?" I think for a second. "Why don't Doug and I stay and take care of the Horsemen until you get back? I'll work on the party while I wait for you."

He nods and wipes an eye. "Jo tried making some calls for it the last few days. She could barely gather enough oxygen to be heard over the phone."

"I'll figure it out. You go. Give her a big hug for me."

He blinks and nods, still looking shell-shocked. "I will. Thanks. I'll call you later."

He fishes his keys out of his pocket, and he's gone in the SUV, the dogs trotting after his car until he turns at the end of the drive-way. I forgot to even ask where Jo was hospitalized.

I watch him go, thinking about what I saw. Surely Tania was comforting Travis after learning Jo was in the hospital. Still, I can't scrub the snapshot of their kiss from my brain. It wasn't exactly platonic. But it doesn't matter right now. Travis is hurting; I have to help.

I carry Doug inside. He's scowling at the Horsemen, and without Travis here, I don't dare introduce them myself. Doug will have to spend the evening in a back bedroom. Hopefully he doesn't run across Sunny.

I pick a door, and end up in Travis's room. Jeans and man-sized scrubs sprawl on the unmade bed. The dogs follow me, sniffing at the bedroom door after I shut Doug in. Once he's settled, I take a look around. Dirty dishes sit on the counter and fill the sink, take-out containers lie open on the table, and papers are scattered everywhere. From the smell, I gather Travis got home too late for one of the dogs to do its business outside.

I get to work. First, I locate the source of the smell. A small pile of poop hides in the corner of the living room—Dex looks guilty. I find a bag and clean it up. After that, I throw away the food, load and start the dishwasher, and clean the countertops. I police the chairs, blankets, and clothes lying around, and then try to sort the mail and other paperwork into piles. Finally, I settle at the table to see where Jo left things.

Jo. My heart hurts thinking I might never see her warm brown eyes again. Even though I haven't known her long, she left an impression. Her warmth, her love for animals, and most of all for her grandson, is painfully obvious. She looks sixty at most. This is too soon.

The Horsemen settle at my feet while I work. Jo must have known she wouldn't be able to finish, because she left detailed notes on what still needs to be done. There aren't a ton of big things left, only details, like creating a chart of which booth would go where in the park, and suggesting songs for the DJ. I leave as little for Travis to do as possible. The party is in two weeks, and I don't know how much time he'll have to focus on it.

At around nine o'clock, I feed all the dogs out of a huge tin of dry dog food I find in the bottom of the pantry, borrowing a bowl for Doug. Then I step outside to check on Chuck.

The moon is a sliver, so I can barely make out his hulking shape in the corner of the pen. I scoop several pitchforks of grass and dump them in, like Travis did, then I stand, arms on the fence and watch as the bison moves closer. His tiny hooves don't make as much noise as an animal that heavy should, but his breathing gives him away.

"Hey, Chuck," I say softly.

He snorts, shakes his massive head, and reaches down for a bite of hay, crunching it between his teeth.

The last time I stood here, only a few weeks ago, Jo stood beside me. She'd deteriorated so fast. My heart aches for her and for Travis.

As if he senses I'm thinking about him, my phone vibrates with a text. *Thanks for staying, but it's going to be a long night here. I'll call you later.*

I stare at my phone, wishing I could actually talk to him, but he's busy, and Jo needs him. I'll have to wait. I open the Lyft app and arrange to be picked up.

Doug sits quietly in my lap all the way home. Maybe the stress of the Four Horsemen lurking outside the bedroom door was too much for him. Outside our apartment building, I let Doug sniff around. Suddenly he drags me to the door of the building and onto the elevator.

"What, Dougie? What is it?" I ask.

He yips impatiently, scratching the metal doors until they slide open at our floor. Then he pulls me to the apartment door. Confused by his excitement, I open it.

Avery and Jason sit on the couch talking to a third person, a guy. Someone tall, blonde, and male. Avery looks tense, her expression sour. Out of the corner of my eye, I spot a familiar suitcase.

I push the door fully open and drop the leash. Doug rushes in and leaps joyfully into the arms . . . of Tim.

Chapter Twenty

I freeze, staring at my *ex*-boyfriend. The guy who's supposed to be in Indonesia, not standing in my living room looking like he swam the whole way back.

Tim's hair is mussed, his eyes are bloodshot, and his clothes—shorts and a Golden State shirt—are rumpled. As rumpled as my heart suddenly feels.

Tim's eyes are on me, but his arms are full of Doug, who's suddenly having a day right up there with the time he scarfed down half a meat-and-cheese tray left unattended on the coffee table. He squirms, squeals, and his tail wags at light speed.

Tim tries to put Doug down after a minute, but he immediately starts hopping up and down on Tim's legs, tongue lolling, until he's picked back up.

When his hysterics finally die down, Tim looks at me. "How's it going, Mel?"

I shake my head, trying to clear the fog of shock. "How's it *going*? What are you *doing* here?"

"I came for a visit." He scratches Doug's head, then buries his face in the wrinkles on top. "Didn't I Lil' Dougie? I came to see you two." He's rewarded with several wet slurps on the face.

I glance at Avery, who's watching Tim with a sneer. She throws me a look like *what the hell?* Did she think I knew about this and didn't tell her?

"Jace, why don't we go grab some, uh, coffee," she says. "I'm sure these two need to . . . talk."

"But Tim just got here," Jason starts. He looks at Avery's face. "Yeah, uh, okay. Good to see you, man. We'll catch up later." He pats me on the shoulder as they go past and out the door.

I still haven't moved. I'm sure it's starting to look weird, but I can't believe Tim's here.

His face scrunches. "You okay? Did I shock you that much?"

Yes! Of course you did! You're supposed to be halfway around the world rubbing shoulders with the rich and powerful, not standing in my living room, cradling my . . . our . . . dog.

I gesture to the couch. Okay, I can move. Getting my voice to work is another story. I manage to squeak out, "Do you want to sit down?"

"Sure, thanks. How about another beer? I've been missing good old Colorado-brewed IPAs."

I almost forgot he likes IPAs best. I hate them. Too hoppy. I find one in the fridge, pour it in a glass, and grab a bag of pretzels out of the pantry.

His big body is spread out on the couch. I'd forgotten how much real estate he takes up. Travis is shorter and slimmer. Doug lies on his back in Tim's lap, thoroughly enjoying the petting and scratching he's providing. Happiness radiates from his upside-down smile to his kicking feet.

Okay, Doug's happy Tim's here. How do I feel? Now that the shock's fading a bit, I'm mostly bewildered and exhausted. It's been a long night. I collapse into a chair. Dog hair, and not only Doug's, covers my jeans.

Tim takes a long drink, finishing with a satisfied smack of the lips.

"So, what are you doing here?" The question comes out sharper than I mean for it to.

He blinks. "I told you. I'm here to see you and Doug."

I hold my hand to the side, palm up. "But why? And why didn't you let me know you were coming?"

Tim puts Doug down beside him, then leans forward to rest his arms on his legs. Damn. He looks so good. Even better than when he left. All sunshine and blue skies and long, tan limbs. He's like the personification of those Corona commercials where relaxed, happy people drink beer on the beach in the shade of a palm tree. Add your own seagull sounds. He even smells like salt and lime.

"I got the funding," he says. "For Global Baller. That investor I told you about? Karen? She committed to helping me get it started." His eyes glow with excitement.

"Wow, that's great." I try to muster more enthusiasm, but all I can picture is the woman I saw in the corner of his computer screen a while ago during one of his Skype calls. She was older, but pretty, blond, and obviously ridiculously wealthy. Now she has a name, too. Karen. In my memory, Tim's bedsheets move.

His expression slumps a little when I don't jump to my feet and fist-pump with joy, but he presses on. "So . . . this means I can come home."

"Oh."

Doug squeezes himself between Tim's tented arm and leg and tosses his head, trying to get him to pet him again.

"Oh? That's it?" Tim makes a frustrated sound. "Amelia, every single time we talked, you asked when I was coming back. I thought this would make you happy."

He's right. I did. I push down thoughts of his Balinese bed sheets and put some effort into my smile.

"I am happy for you, Tim. I'm thrilled Global Ballers is getting the funding it deserves. You've worked so hard to get it going. Are you back for good now?"

"No, just for a few days." He's furiously scratching Doug, who's loving it. "As soon as I got the yes from Karen, I booked the flight here. But I have to go back on Sunday to finish things up. Another few weeks, maybe."

I look at a faded stain on the carpet, probably caused by you-know-who. "And where are you staying?"

He glances at me and a smooth smile slides across his face. "I was hoping I could stay here. On the couch. Or wherever."

My brain swells with all the unexpected information. A few days? A few weeks? Or wherever?

I'd finally started divorcing myself from the dream of Tim. Now he's sitting on my couch and soon to be back in Denver.

Tim slides himself and Doug over on the couch, leaving room beside him. "Why are you sitting so far away? Come on over and tell me how you've been."

He rests his left arm across the back of the couch. It's an invitation, and a tempting one. An old, familiar thrill of anticipation runs through my body. A month ago, maybe less, I would have scurried over and snuggled up against him, happy as Doug. Even now, the loneliness I've felt, that yearning for the connection I'd lost, pushes me to go to him.

But then why are my heart racing and palms sweating like I'm in danger?

I stay put.

"I still don't understand. I just talked to you a few days ago. You didn't say anything about being close to getting the investment, or that you were even thinking about coming home. What changed?"

Tim takes a pull off his beer before answering. "You didn't really give me the chance to tell you, did you?" He looks hurt for a second. "Look Amelia, after the last time we talked, I realized that maybe I haven't been fair to you. You've been really sweet and supportive all this time, taking good care of Lil' Dougie, keeping in touch even though we broke things off before I left. You've really gone above and beyond."

I love how he makes it sound like we decided jointly to break up, instead of owning the way it actually was.

The truth is, I let him pull the walls of my life down when he left, and I only had Avery, Jason, and Doug to help me rebuild. It's taken me months to reframe and drywall. He's not waltzing back in that easily.

I close my eyes. "I'm sorry if I'm being slow, but what is it, exactly, that you want now?"

I open my eyes again, and his blue eyes burn into mine. "You, Amelia, and Doug. I want what we had back."

Those words. I'd been dreaming of him saying those words for so long. Now he's here, in my living room, saying them, and they're confusing the hell out of me. Don't I want him back, too?

I rub my eyes. My brain drags with fatigue. "It's been a long week. I'm exhausted. Seeing you is a surprise—"

"A good one, I hope."

"Yes, a good one. I'm happy to see you, and I'm so glad you got the money you need for Global Ballers. But . . . I need to think about this. And I need to sleep." When I stand, Doug leaps to his feet, tail curling.

Tim looks disappointed, but he nods. "Okay. So, can I stay?"

A spiteful part of me wants to say no. He can go find a hotel. But Doug is watching every move he makes with a worshipful expression.

"Sure."

Tim stands, that sexy smile back on his face. He walks toward me, but I step back.

"On the couch. I'll get you some blankets and a pillow."

I smile at the disappointed look on his face as I gather a pillow and old comforter from the linen closet and bring them back to the living room.

Tim lays them on the couch and puts his hands in his pockets as I again step back. Doug rubs up against his legs, then circles around mine like a cat. He looks from him to me and barks.

"Well, good night," I say. "Congratulations again."

He holds his arms out. "Can I at least get a hug? I did travel over twenty-four hours to see you."

I hesitate. *It's only a hug.* "Sure."

I step into the circle, and he pulls me against him. I'm stiff and uncomfortable at first, but after a few seconds, I relax.

Tim's hugs are heaven—soft, lingering, and very, very warm. He pulls me in to his still-hard belly and hips. Lust and longing sizzle through me as I become aware that he really has missed me. Parts of him, at least.

His lips touch my forehead, and he whispers my name. Slowly, he tips my chin up and kisses me. Once, twice, and then with conviction.

All-out war flames between my body and my brain. I want him to stop. I want him to never stop! While my own parts take sides, I stand very still, reveling in the feeling of being wanted again.

And equally sick with guilt that I'm kissing Tim while Jo and Travis are at the hospital.

I don't know what else might have happened, if Avery and Jason hadn't opened the door right then. Tim and I step apart, while Doug barks at them.

"Sorry." If Avery's tone got any flatter, I could use it as a Frisbee.

I tug the hem of my shirt down, not realizing Tim had been creeping it up. "No, it's okay. We're going to bed."

Jason grins, and Avery looks like she might shake me.

My cheeks boil. "I. *I'm* going to bed. Tim's going to sleep on the couch, if that's okay with you two."

"Sure. That's fine." Avery storms into the kitchen and starts rummaging in the fridge. I think she's waiting to make sure I go to my room alone.

"Well, good night." I can't meet Tim's eyes.

"Night. It's really good to see you in real life again, Amelia."

His lips linger against my cheek. A new skirmish breaks out in my body, but I squelch the rebellion and march the troops to my room. Doug trots after me, but when he realizes Tim isn't coming, he stops in the hallway, looking at me, then him.

As I take off my makeup and get undressed, I can't help listening to Tim unzip his suitcase, brush his teeth in my bathroom, and then pause outside my door. I even hear Doug squirming around on his back, grunting like he does when he wants attention. I bite my lip and wait, deciding what to say if Tim knocks or comes in.

After a very long pause, he goes back to the living room. The TV comes on at a low volume. He likes to watch television before bed, while I like to read. When we were together, I'd try reading for a few pages, but I could never concentrate, so I'd give up and watch what he was watching. I'd forgotten that, too.

As I drift off in a muddled cloud of emotions, I hear Doug sigh from his new post in the hallway, halfway between us.

Chapter Twenty-One

That night, I dream of Travis.

It's not a particularly racy dream, not like a few others I've had in the last few weeks. In this dream, we're back by the river, fully clothed, and kissing.

His lips move against mine, his skin smells amazing, like oranges and leather, and his hands are tangled lightly in my hair. I dive in to that kiss, dive in to him.

"Amelia," he whispers. "I want you." His eyes pin me, and the chalk in his voice makes me shiver. "Forget Tim. Be with me."

I open my eyes to tell him I will, but he's changed. His fine features are gone, replaced by black and tan wrinkles. His eyes are wet and droopy. And the orange and leather scent is now stinky dog breath. Doug is curled on the pillow beside me, his face an inch from mine.

Still half asleep, I rear back and fall off the rock—the bed—sending my lamp flying with an elbow. Doug leaps to his feet, barking, and a few seconds later, Tim, Avery, and Jason rush in.

The guys crack up when they see me on the ground surrounded by broken chunks of ceramic base, the lampshade overturned beside me.

"Are you okay?" Avery asks with a croaky voice. Her hair is a mess and she's clutching a robe around her.

"Yes." I grumble and rub my elbow, annoyed that Tim's snickering as he helps me up. I'm sure I look funny, but it hurt. The clock says it's eight. Way too early for a Saturday morning, but there was no going back to sleep now. "Sorry I woke you all."

Jason rubs his stubbly cheek. "I'm getting coffee. Anyone want some?" We all raise our hands, and he shuffles to the kitchen.

Tim yawns and stretches. His thin T-shirt reveals that his muscles are still in all the right places. Still feeling the dreamy effects of Travis's kiss, I look away.

"I'm going to be seriously jet lagged all day anyway, and since I'm flying back tomorrow night, I might as well stay that way," he says.

"Wait, you're leaving tomorrow?" Avery asks him.

She texted me twice last night from her room, wanting the scoop about why Tim was here, but I was honestly too worn out to answer.

"He's going back to wrap things up, then he's coming home. He got the funding."

Avery's parade of expressions from relief to horror is sort of funny.

"That's . . . great?" she says, question mark included.

"Thanks." Tim slings an arm around me. "I'll be taking Amelia and Doug back off your hands in a month or so."

"What?" Avery and I say in unison.

He smiles at me. "I thought you could look for a new apartment for us while I'm finishing up there, maybe arrange to get my stuff delivered from the storage unit, and you and Doug can move in whenever you guys are ready. Right, my man?"

He drops to a knee. Doug growls and chases his hands, gnawing them gently.

Avery takes the opportunity to eye-stab me. Utterly confused, I can only shake my head.

"Hey, since we're up, want to take Lil' Dougie for a walk?" Tim asks me.

I sigh. "Why not."

Travel mugs of coffee in hand, we meander around sleepy Saturday morning downtown streets, passing only the occasional jogger or breakfast seeker. Tim rambles about his plans for Global Baller now that he's got cash to get it going, plans that include plenty of long stints traveling internationally to start delivering the balls to impoverished children once production starts.

He moves on to where I should look for an apartment, how many rooms and square feet, and what amenities he's hoping to have.

"I'll send you the deposit and first month's rent as soon as you find it," he adds quickly, as if money is my only concern. "And of course they need to allow dogs, right, Dougie?"

Doug lifts his leg and pees on a light post, apparently perfectly satisfied with the plan. And I have to admit, part of me wants to go along with it, too. At one point, Tim takes my hand in his, rubbing it lightly with his thumb, like he used to. And I can almost fall back in to the fantasy. Almost.

But early on in the walk, we pass the rock where I kissed Travis. I stare at it as we pass, my thoughts and feelings in a jumble. I would love to believe Tim experienced a sudden, 180-degree change from less than a week ago, but I can't quite make it work in my head.

When we get home, I text Travis about Jo, with no answer. Looking for news, I even hide in my room to call a few hospitals that they might have gone to, but citing patient confidentiality, no one will tell me if she's there. A terrible feeling grows as the day wears on. How is Jo? Why hasn't Travis responded?

I know he must be with her, and I realize I'm not exactly at the top of his list to keep informed, but couldn't he spare me two seconds for a quick text back? Is it because of Tania? Or am I being totally shallow?

Yes, Travis kissed Tania, but I kissed Tim. What's the difference? Travis should have all the support he can get right now. And instead of being there with him, holding his hand, I'm holding Tim's.

Disgust seeps through me.

Tim and I eat lunch at home. I automatically make his favorite veggie sandwich with avocado, lettuce, tomato, and slices of those sweet mini peppers, with fruit and yogurt on the side. We take Doug to the dog park, and that night meet up at a bar with some of Tim's friends, people I haven't seen in months.

I ask and answer questions, laugh at jokes, and say the right things, but I'm going through the motions. I've felt almost detached from my body since I came through the door last night to find Tim in our living room.

Saturday bleeds in to Sunday with no word from Travis. I'm so desperate find out how Jo is, I decide to get a Lyft out to his house as soon as Tim leaves for the airport.

Finally, finally, Tim zips up his bag and says good-bye to Avery and Jason. My body shivers with pent-up tension. I'm looking back at him as I open the door to let him out. Which means I don't see the bedraggled person standing in the hallway, fist raised to knock, until I almost run into him. His hair is loose, his eyes are glassy, and he smells like he hasn't showered or changed in a few days.

"Travis!" I say. "Oh . . . no." From the pain in his eyes, I know instantly that Jo's gone.

"Amelia, I—" His gaze focuses behind me, on Tim, and his expression flattens. He steps back.

I don't have words to comfort him, or to explain why Tim is in my apartment, so I say nothing. I hope the tears in my eyes show how I feel about Jo.

When I don't introduce him, Tim reaches past me to shake Travis's hand. "Travis . . . Brewer? Doug's vet? Amelia said you made house calls, but on Sundays? That's good service, man." His tone is mildly sarcastic.

"That's me." Travis's voice is raw and scratchy. Hurt is woven through his words.

From behind Tim, Doug growls.

The corner of Travis's lips lift briefly. He clears his throat. "Well, I can see Doug's doing fine for now, so I'll go." He throws a look full of jealousy and pain at me that pierces my heart.

I grab his arm. "Travis, wait. Please. What about Jo?"

"She passed this morning. The funeral is Wednesday."

He tugs his arm out of my hands, and hurries down the hall to the elevator as fast as he can go without actually running.

Chapter Twenty-Two

Before he leaves, Tim assures me he'll be back soon. He tries to kiss me, but I turn my face away at the last second.

I'm still numb from the news about Jo. I knew she was ill, and fragile, but it's still awful. And I can't erase the memory of the suffering I saw in Travis's eyes.

More than anything, I wish he hadn't had to tell me she'd died with Tim there. He didn't deserve that.

As soon as Tim disappears through the elevator doors, I call Travis's cell phone. He doesn't answer, so I leave a rambling message full of apologies and platitudes. Hopefully my sincerity came through. I don't know.

Heartsick, I take Doug out for a walk to think. The weekend was a whirlwind, and I can't sort out how I feel.

Tim wants me back, I guess. My relationship with Travis, so promising a few days ago, seems uncertain now.

And Jo is gone. As I walk, tears slide down my cheeks for a woman I wish I could have known much better.

At least Doug is happy. He doesn't bark at other dogs or growl as men go by. His tail is erect and his trot jaunty. So long as the pug is pleased, all is right with the world.

Only, it's not. Not at all. I text and call Travis several more times with no response, then decide I'm probably annoying him and stop. If he wants to talk, he'll call.

Jason makes dinner, but I can't eat. I sit on my bed petting Doug, who's curled up in my lap. Avery comes in and sits down.

"Amelia, *what* is going on with Tim? And what happened with Travis? What did he say when he came?"

I tell her about Jo, and the hurt in his eyes when he saw me with Tim. "We didn't promise each other anything, but . . ." I struggle to put it into words. "Just being together felt like a promise. You know? With Travis, I feel like I'm front and center in his mind. With Tim, I sometimes felt like an afterthought."

Avery pats my leg. "Doesn't that pretty much tell you all you need to know?"

My shoulders sag. "Maybe, but Travis hasn't answered a single text or phone call since the night I went to his house. I've tried to explain on voicemail why Tim was there, but it comes out so lame. If I can't get him to talk to me, doesn't that mean I don't really have a choice now?"

"You don't know that. His grandmother died. He's grieving. Maybe he needs time. You can give him that."

I wince at my next thought, knowing how it will sound. "But what if I give him the time he needs, and lose Tim?"

Her expression sours. "Being without Tim didn't kill you. You can do it again if Travis says no."

I grab my phone and show her a picture of myself that I texted Kenny after Tim broke up with me. I'm greasy, pale, and my hair looks like something from a sewer nested in it. I'd been crying on and off for days.

"Remember her?"

She snorts. "Hard to forget."

"I don't know if I can go through that again, with Travis *or* Tim." At least with Tim, I've already been through it. The pain would be familiar. With Travis, it would be fresh, new, and horrible.

Avery shakes her head. "I get it. But that's the rub of being in love, Melly. You gotta take the bad with the good. If you aren't ready for that, you aren't ready to be with anyone."

ℰ

I hear from Tim a few times over the next two days, telling me how much he loved seeing me, and how excited he is to get home to Doug and me, and oh, can I be sure the apartment complex has a workout room?

I respond to his questions but not to the love and excitement parts. I don't know what to say.

Without Kenny, the HHB office is colder and lonelier than ever before. Forty doesn't show for the Monday staff meeting because he has walking pneumonia, and Max has the week off, which is lucky for him, because I have some choice words for him. I still haven't responded to his email. What's the point? He's going to do whatever he's going to do.

Wednesday comes, and miraculously, Jim gives me a few hours off to go to Jo's funeral, although it's not long enough to attend the viewing beforehand. If he hadn't let me go, I would have quit. Which kind of makes me wish he'd been a jerk about it.

The cemetery is in West Denver, in a quiet neighborhood south of I-70. I arrive late thanks to traffic, and creep up behind the crowd. And it is a crowd.

I haven't been to many funerals. The ones I have—for a friend in high school who was killed in a car accident, and for my great grandparents—were fifty people at most. At least double that are here to say good-bye to Jo.

Through the crowd, I can only see a sliver of her grave, her coffin waiting to be lowered in, and the priest who's saying a prayer. Who I can see fairly well, is Travis.

He's devastatingly handsome in a black suit and crisp white shirt, standing beside the grave, hands crossed in front of him. His hair is pulled back neatly, and from the stiff set of his body, he's barely holding himself together.

My breath catches. I want to push through all the people and run to him, throw my arms around him, and tell him I'm here if he wants me. To stand close to him and be his support, like he's been mine. He looks so terribly alone.

And then I spot Tania. Wearing huge black glasses and a fitted suit, she stands a step away from Travis.

Seeing them like that, dressed up and so close together, I realize how much they fit. They grew up together, were childhood sweethearts. They know each other's life stories intimately, and they created a life together, no matter what problems they had. I don't fit in that picture at all.

After a second, the crowd shifts, blocking the thin view I had of them.

The homily drifts to me in snippets. The priest outlines all Jo accomplished in her life, and all the people and places she did good for. I see others nodding as he speaks.

The priest finishes speaking and invites people to come forward to say a few words about Jo. One by one, people speak of her kindness, her generosity. What she did for them that she often didn't take credit for. Old-sounding people, young-sounding people, even one boy who said she made the best chocolate chip cookies ever.

People loved Jo because she touched them in so many small ways. Travis, too. Avery's work improves the environment. When he gets Global Ballers up and running, even Tim will be doing good for kids around the world.

I take stock of my own life as I strain to hear. What have I really done? Who have *I* helped? Who do I want to be, and what do I need to do to become her?

Finally, Travis speaks. His voice is clear, but he sounds exhausted. I slide around people, closer and closer, until I can see and hear him.

"Josephine Mary Brewer—my Jo—was a mother, grandmother, and friend. She loved her family. But what made her remarkable, as you heard today, was how often she thought of others first, even strangers, and did anything she could for them. She had a huge heart and a small ego. She did big things in small ways, whether it was for people or animals, and small as she was, her passing leaves a huge hole in my heart." He pauses and wipes his eyes. I do, too. "Before she died, Jo chose a poem she asked me to read." He pulls out a sheet of paper.

> Years go by, and we go with them, rising and falling
>   through seasons and tides,
> Years go by, and we go with them, our lives spinning
>   while love abides,
> Years go by, and we go with them, slowing, speeding
>   as we're carried along,
> Years go by, and we go with them.
> They end when we end, but the world spins on.

He addresses the crowd, only it feels like he's speaking directly to me.

"Be sure that when your years end and the world spins on, that you've left it a better place, like Jo did."

All around me, people sniffle or outright sob. I search my purse. Why didn't I remember to pack tissues? A woman next to me hands me some.

Travis steps back, and Tania hugs him for a long, long time. The priest ends the service.

People line up to file by the grave and pay their respects to Travis. I follow them, smoothing my hair and navy dress. Clouds darken the sky, and lightning strikes of nerves hit me as I wait my turn.

I stand beside Jo's grave and say a short prayer for her. I don't know if she can hear me, but I feel better for having said it. After several long breaths to calm my nerves, I step up to speak to Travis. Unsure if a hug will be welcome, I stick out my hand to shake his and say how sorry I am.

He looks dazed, like he's not fully there. Smiling robotically, he thanks me for coming. And that's it.

I hesitate, wanting to say and do so much more. But instead I move along to make room for the next mourner.

After work, I drag myself home. Doug tackles me as I come through the door. I take him out for a short walk, then sit with him on the couch, scratching his head, and check my email. Avery forwarded one from the landlord. They found out Doug's living here. He has to go.

My body is hot and swollen, ready to explode. Doug whines and looks up at me, concerned. When I don't move or speak, he nuzzles my hand and puts his chin on my leg, his wrinkles deepening.

Travis won't speak to me. Max reported Doug to animal control. Kenny's gone, and I can't ignore how much I hate my job any longer. Doug and I are being evicted. I gasp in a breath, feeling trapped.

What am I going to do now?

Chapter Twenty-Three

I call and text Travis multiple times the next few days to check on him. He doesn't call back. Going to his house feels too intrusive. And finding a mobile office when it doesn't want to be found is impossible.

Like a lot of the bad news I've gotten lately, his final answer to me comes in an email a week after Jo's funeral.

A bill. Payment in full due for veterinary services rendered. No note, no explanation. No return texts or calls.

I leave work without telling anyone and don't crawl out of bed again for twenty-four hours.

When I don't have any more tears to cry, I pull my laptop out and start searching for apartments for Tim, Doug, and me in earnest.

Chapter Twenty-Four

Early on the morning of the Love & Pets Party, I'm sitting in bed, Doug's head on my lap, eating an entire pint of mocha-chocolate-chip ice cream for breakfast.

Avery bursts in, startling Doug, whose head hits my spoon, flinging drops of ice cream into my face and hair. I snatch up a tissue to wipe my eyes clean and glare at her.

She crosses her arms and scowls right back. "What are you doing, Amelia? Get out of bed."

"Why should I? I don't have anything to do today." Doug settles back down, wary eyes on my sister.

"What do you mean? Aren't you going to the party?"

"No."

"I don't get what's going on with you. You helped Travis plan this thing. Why wouldn't you go?"

How did she even know when the party was supposed to be? Then I remembered: I put a flyer on the fridge before everything went to hell. I lay my head back on the headboard.

"He doesn't want me there, and I can prove it." I pull up the emailed invoice on my phone and show it to her.

"What? He's not supposed to charge you for the work he did?"

"Of course he can! But after we kissed *twice*, I thought a little personal note or explanation about why he hasn't even texted me back might be nice. I know he's hurting since losing Jo, but this is . . . just wrong!" I drop the phone.

Avery sighs. "You have a point there. But look at you." She throws up a hand. "Eating ice cream in bed at eight thirty in the morning with your dog? I can't stand seeing you like this. After spending time with Travis, you *glowed*. I haven't seen you that happy since before you met Tim."

Before I met Tim? I shake my head. Doug is licking my spoon, so I put it and the ice cream carton down on the bedside table.

"Avery, I tried to talk to Travis. Repeatedly. He obviously doesn't want to see or hear from me. So I'm moving on with the guy who does."

Her face turns lava red. "Going back to Tim is not moving on. It's rocketing in reverse."

With an obvious effort to calm down, she sits on the edge of my bed and puts a hand on the lump that's my foot under the covers.

I try to explain. "He said he wishes he never broke up with me. That he missed Doug and me. He wants us back. And we want him, too, right, Dougie?" I smush his face and he smiles, his teeth peeking through his dark lips.

Avery's hands clench. "Okay, Melly, you need some straight talk today. Tim is . . ." She considers her words. "An *asshole*."

"Avery!"

"Listen up. First, he tells you he has great news. He's leaving for Indonesia. But you have to move out because he's giving up your apartment. He thinks you should see other people while he's gone, and could you please keep his dog for him?"

I have to admit her impression of Tim's slick sales voice is spot on.

"*Then*, he asks you to sit at home alone on Friday nights for months so he can talk to his *dog* and tell you how fantastic Indonesia is." She paces across the room and back. "*Then*, the minute you tell him he can go drown himself in the spectacular

Indian Ocean"—she's been eavesdropping on our weekly conversa-
tions, I can tell—"he shows up at our apartment like he never left,
saying he wants you back. By the way, could you please find
another apartment for him before he gets back?"

She presses her temples. "It was everything I could do not to
kick him out of here myself. But not you! No, you take him back!
You're finding him an apartment! And you're giving up on the one
guy since Ben Haverson in the tenth grade who I think could be
genuinely good for you. You need to find your spine, Amelia. Right
damn now."

Her anger pins me to the headboard. When tears well, Avery's
expression turns to sympathy.

"I'm sorry, Melly. That was harsh. I just," she grabs my hands.
"I want you to be happy so bad. And I don't think Tim will ever
make you happy. He'll make himself happy, and if you want to
come along for that ride, that's great. Until he decides someone
else makes him happier."

Hearing it like that—the brutal truth—I know she's right. Tim
is charming, handsome, intelligent . . . and completely self-
centered. When I was with him, I convinced myself that what
made him happy made me happy, too.

She smooths my hair and softens her voice. "And another thing.
Why are you still working a dead-end job for a law practice that
you hate? Kenny's gone, Mel. What's keeping you there?"

"I don't know what else to do." I bury my fingers in Doug's
soft, tan folds.

Avery points at him. "You love animals, and they love you.
Why not try working with them, like Travis?"

Weird, Travis said the same thing. I do love animals. And I had
a great day with Travis and his patients. It wasn't only that I
enjoyed spending time with him, either. Helping the animals with
their problems and comforting their worried owners was so much
more rewarding than any work I've done up to now.

"I'd have to go back to school, and I can't afford that."

"If I knew it was what you really wanted, you know I'd help pay for it."

"You help me so much already."

"There are ways to pay for school. That's just an excuse."

She's right. Of course I could go back to school. And I could break up with Tim—again. And move on from the disastrous relationship with Travis. Find a place for Doug and me to live. The question is—where do I start? I feel paralyzed.

"I don't know what to do."

"What do you *want* to do? Put your big-girl panties on and decide."

What do I want?

Doug gazes at me. We've come a long way together, he and I. Before we moved in, he'd only sit with Tim. He followed him everywhere he went. Now he follows me around. He watches me. We can take walks without him lunging at men. And he's not *as* destructive as he was.

Everything began to change for the better when we met Travis. He was the key. Whether it was Pug Paradise, the little suggestions like taking Doug on more walks, or spending extra time together, Travis did everything he could to support us. And I developed feelings for him in return. I can't give up on our relationship until I look him in the eye and find out once and for all where we stand.

My body tingles and my heart hammers as I think about finding the words to say to him. But this is the truth that whispers in my soul: *Travis is who I want.*

I shimmy out of bed and jump up. Inspired by my burst of energy, Doug grabs the corner of the comforter to show it who's boss.

"Where are you going?" Avery asks.

"To the first annual Love & Pets Party!" I grab the nearest pair of jeans and start pulling them on.

Avery turns me toward the mirror. I'm covered in dried splatters of ice cream. "Shower. I'll drive you. I'm not missing this."

I hug her like it's the last time I'll see her and run to the computer.

"Now what?" she asks, sounding baffled.

"I'm making my first big-girl panty decision and sending Tim an email."

She squints suspiciously. "Saying what?"

"That I don't want to get back together. That I'm sorry I didn't tell him when he was here. And that he can find his own stupid apartment. I'm giving myself no outs, Aves. No matter what Travis decides I'm not going to let myself crawl back to Tim." I quickly type the email and hit Send.

She hoots. "Amen, sister. Only you should dump him over Skype on a Friday night. Jerk."

With Doug bouncing around my feet, I run for the shower, elated but also feeling a little sick. What if Travis won't speak to me? I can't let him reject me until I have my say. I'll *make* him hear me out.

I only hope that it's not too little, or too late.

Chapter Twenty-Five

My leg bounces up and down the whole way out to the park as Doug whines through his muzzle beside me on the back seat. Avery and Jason are up front. She keeps glancing back in the mirror at us.

"You sure it's a good idea to bring him?"

"It's an event for pets."

"But he's still kind of aggressive, right? Are you going to keep that muzzle on him the whole time?"

"I guess so. Hopefully he'll behave. He did great the last time we were at Pug Paradise."

The truth is, having Doug with me gives me courage. I'm doing this for him, too. His connection to Tim is as unhealthy as mine, and it's time for both of us to cut the leash.

The party is in full swing when we arrive. The food trucks I arranged are here. Tents featuring sponsoring pet-supply companies and pet adoption groups line the sidewalk. The DJ I contacted is pumping out the music.

Everywhere I look, people and their pets cruise around, checking out the tents. They're mostly dogs, but I see a cat on a leash, carriers with pocket pets, and even one snake around someone's neck—reminding me of the massage I gave to Mr. Stricture.

Kids and puppies frolic in the grass while their adults stand nearby, eating and chatting. With the mountains in the distance, and sun shining in the late August bluebird summer sky, the scene couldn't be more perfect.

The Love & Pets RV sits in the center of it all. Travis must have gotten permission to drive it up on a large cement area adjacent to the grass.

The whole time Tim was in town I felt numb, like I was going through the motions. For the first time since I heard Jo died, my body fizzes with nerves and excitement. I'd see Travis soon.

What if he's not interested anymore? What if Jo's death, or Tania, or seeing me with Tim, changed the connection between us? What if he doesn't feel the way I do about him? I don't have any answers, but it's high time I found out.

Doug keeps trying to see around me as I let him out of the car on his leash. His ears and tail are perked, and the ridge of hair along his back rises. He growls, just for a second, as a dog walks past. Maybe it was a mistake to bring him, like Avery said, but too late now. I keep a tight grip on his leash.

My sister hugs me. "Are you ready?"

I swallow and nod.

"Good luck, Melly. It's all going to work out. You'll see."

Jason gives me a quick side hug. "You got this, Amelia."

I take a deep breath and head toward the RV. The door's closed; he must already be seeing patients. But sitting outside is a folding table manned by a woman in a pug suit.

"Brenda!"

Doug yanks me toward her. I pull him back, until I see Daisy is under the table. Brenda and I smile as they greet each other, tails wagging furiously. He whines softly and stays close to his friend, circling her.

"Well. Looks like they're glad to see each other," Brenda says.

"And I'm glad to see you. Are you here looking for people to adopt the puglets?"

"Oh no, that bunch is already with their forever families—all except for Daisy here."

"No one good enough for her?" I scratch the rolls on her head.

A secretive smile passes over Brenda's face. "Don't worry about this girl. I have a line on a high-quality family for her. No, I'm here for Dr. Travis. Checking patients in and out, collecting payments." She points to a tablet and connected credit card reader on the table.

Jo would've done this for him, I'm sure. He must have asked Brenda, instead. I should have thought of that and volunteered a week ago. I was too wrapped up in my own misery, my own problems to think about what he needed. On the other hand, he could've returned a text or phone call. Every time I think about that, I get mixed up again. I glance at the closed door of the RV, the leash slick in my hands.

"Is he in there?"

"Yup. With the cutest Bernese mountain dog mix you've ever seen. They're called Berners, and his name is Bunson." She laughs like she cracked a good joke. "Bunson. Didn't you take chemistry? Bunson Berner?"

I laugh politely, but I can't really focus. I'm so scared I can barely breathe. I need to talk to Travis before I lose my nerve.

"Hey Brenda, do you want a break? I can take over for you here."

She picks up the tablet gingerly, like it's made of gold. "You know how to work these things?"

I tell her I do.

"Well. Thanks very much, Amelia. Daisy and I will go check out the booths, eh, Daisy girl?" Daisy's eyes stay on Doug. "Schedule's right there on top when you turn the thing on."

"I got it. Thanks. Enjoy the party."

People turn all the way around to stare at Brenda as she goes by. Doug pulls on his leash, trying to follow Daisy as she prances off, too. When she finally disappears in the crowd, he settles under the table next to half-full bowl of water. Looking around, I realize there are bowls of water all over the park. Jo must have arranged for them. She would have loved to see all this.

I check Travis's schedule. A rabbit named Ernest with a suspected ear infection is next up, followed by a turtle with a breathing problem, and several more puppy vaccinations. I recognize the last patient on the list: Beatrix. Her cat Fluffernutter has a possible urinary tract infection. With all those cats, she must have one or two a week with problems to see Travis about. A price list next to the machine tells me he's charging next to nothing for his services today. Surely Beatrix will pay full price, though. She's good for it.

As the minutes tick by, my anxiety grows. People stop by, curious about Travis's practice, and I answer what questions I can. As I finish with one, I'm thrilled to see some familiar faces.

"Kenny! Ruston! How was PV?"

"Breathtaking!" Ruston gushes. "Our hotel was adorable, and the food was stupendous."

"Good weather," Kenny says calmly. An older dark-skinned woman carrying a tiny, shaking Chihuahua walks with them.

"You must be Kenny's mother. I'm so glad to finally meet you," I say to her. "And this has to be the famous Chi-Chi."

"It is." She beams.

"I thought you weren't coming," I say to Kenny.

"Mama wanted to come support your vet and his party. I want to meet *him*." Kenny, his expression as flat as ever, raises an eyebrow.

"And Chi-Chi loves to look at all the animals. Don't you?" Ruston scratches the dog's walnut sized head. Chi-Chi's tiny pink tongue shoots out to lick Ruston's hand.

"What do you think of the party?" I ask them.

People are browsing the booths, gathering freebies, kids transform into tigers and butterflies after visiting the face painter, and a woman twists multicolored balloons into animal shapes as fast as she can. The DJ plays a pretty good mix of hip-hop, pop, alternative, and country.

"It's a perfect summer event," Ruston says.

"Dr. Travis said you helped plan it," Kenny's mother says. I wonder what else he told her about me.

"Yes, ma'am. But a lot of it was Jo's work—Travis's grandmother." I pause, sadness slapping me all over again. "Were you able to meet her?"

She shakes her head. "No. And I was very sorry to hear that she passed. I know it tore him up, just like it did my Kenny when my own mama died a few years ago."

Kenny smiles at his mother and squeezes her shoulder. An actual, full smile. I'd never heard about his grandmother dying, but that was Kenny. He wasn't one to share much of anything personal. That was my job.

As for Travis, I wish I could say I knew how Jo's death affected him.

I grab Kenny's hand. "Wait, wasn't this your first week? How's law school?"

Ruston groans. "He's been there for like three days and he's already studying even *more* hours than before. Can you believe it?" Kenny's mother pats her son's face proudly.

We chat for a few minutes about their trip and Kenny's classes, but I tense as a girl walks up with her father, her arms full of a gorgeous brown rabbit that looks just like a chocolate Easter bunny. It's almost time for Ernest's appointment, which means Travis and I will come eye to eye soon—for better or worse.

"We'll come back by when things slow down," Kenny says. "Let's get Chi-Chi some of those biscuits, Mama." He puts an arm around her, and Ruston waves good-bye to me.

I greet the girl, whose name is Jemima, and her father. Ernest's nose twitches, his eyes on Doug, who's straining to get a closer look.

Finally, the door to the RV opens, and a guy with an adorable lump of black, brown, and white puppy in his arms steps out.

"Thanks again, Doc," he says.

"Don't forget to call and make an appointment for Bunson's

next round of vaccinations," Travis says from the door. He smiles, but his face freezes as he sees me. He looks thinner, with puffy bags under his eyes.

I stand, knocking my chair over, and Doug stiffens. Anything I thought I might say leaks out of my brain.

"Amelia. What are you—?"

I hold a shaky hand out to his patients. "Ernest is here to see you, Doctor. He might have an ear infection, poor guy."

Travis stares at me, and I stare back. Emotions war on his face. I can't say how I look. But inside, I'm pleading with him to let me stay. *Give me a chance. Don't send me away.*

Looking between us with confusion, the girl's father clears his throat.

Travis blinks and turns to them. "Right. Come on in, Ernest. And it's Jemima, right? It's good to have you all back."

He glances at me as he closes the door. The intensity of the look makes goose bumps break out along my arms. He has something to say, I can tell, but it will have to wait. That's fine. I have something to say, too.

I sit at the table for the next hour and a half, checking patients in and out. Avery and Jason bring me a drink and a bowl from Benny's, but I'm too nervous to eat. They take Doug for a walk and to get some treats, then return him.

Every time Travis opens the door, he stares at me a few moments longer, while I smile tentatively and introduce the next patient.

Carrying a small, soft-sided kennel, Bea hurries over a few minutes before her appointment. Her hair is in a messy high bun, and she's wearing a T-shirt with a curled-up cat in a chair on it. This one says *It's a dog eat dog world. Better to just stay home.*

"Apologize to Dr. Travis for me, but Fluffernutter is done—I need to take her home. I'll have to reschedule with him."

I peek inside the carrier at the mottled white and black cat. She's mewing repeatedly, her green eyes wide. Doug jumps to his feet when he hears her, knocking the table leg and almost tipping the soda Avery brought me onto the tablet.

I steady the drink and grab his collar to keep him from going for Bea's cat. "No problem. I'll let him know."

As she rushes down the sidewalk toward the full parking lot, she avoids eye contact and leaves space between herself and anyone she passes. Funny girl.

I open the tablet, delete her name, and enter new information into the now-available appointment slot. When the RV door opens again, I stand, holding Doug under one arm.

Travis looks around. "Who's next?"

I swallow hard. "This is my dog, Doug. He has some attachment issues, I think. Can we talk about it?"

Travis plays with the handle of the RV door. Finally, he steps back.

"Come on in."

Chapter Twenty-Six

On wobbly legs, I lead Doug up the steps and into the RV. He's still muzzled, so I take the leash off once we're inside. He sniffs around, intrigued by the smells of previous patients, but he shies away from Travis.

"So, my dog has this problem," I say, my voice higher than normal. "He's had it for a while, and I think I've only made it worse."

Travis leans against the metal examination table and crosses his arms. "Okay."

"You see, he's very loyal. He . . . he really loved the guy who raised him from a puppy. And when that guy gave him to me to keep, he had a hard time adjusting." I fiddle with the clip end of the leash. "Instead of helping him get over his attachment to the guy, I accidentally encouraged it. Because I was pretty attached, too."

I glance at him. He nods.

"But recently, the guy visited. And I realized he wasn't any good for Doug. He doesn't want Doug all the time. He wants Doug when *he* feels like having him."

"I see. And how does . . . Doug . . . feel about things now?"

We look down at the same time. He's sniffing his way around the edge of the RV, stopping at particularly interesting spots.

"He was hurt. But not as much as I expected."

Travis rubs his chin. "Why do you think that is?"

My face flushes as I think about what to say next. "Because we met someone new. Someone with a big heart who does whatever he can for other people, whenever asked. Someone who's probably really hurting right now, because he lost someone amazing."

Travis takes a moment to speak. "And how do *you* feel about all these changes in Doug?"

I rub my arm. Time to get real. "Honestly, I feel like an idiot for not seeing the problem a long time ago. I should have pushed Tim away sooner, so Doug couldn't keep obsessing about him."

Travis' face twists. "Tim stayed with you—in your apartment—less than two weeks ago. I saw his suitcase as he was leaving. You're saying suddenly something is different?"

Anger roars up in me. "If you'd called or texted me back, I could have explained. I would've told you I didn't invite Tim to stay. He showed up unannounced. And he slept on the couch. Anyway, I'd just seen you looking pretty cozy with Tania at your house. So I'm not sure you have any right to be upset with me about Tim."

He looks confused. "At my house?" His expression clears. "You saw her kiss me."

I wince at the memory. "Yeah. I did. And it didn't look all that platonic. But I stayed and took care of the Horsemen anyway, because you needed me."

"And cleaned up my house . . . which I just realized I never thanked you for." He rubs his neck. "Amelia, that kiss meant nothing. Tania came by to visit Jo and found me going crazy inside, trying to get her stuff together to bring to the hospital. She helped me decide what to pack. I barely knew which end was up, I was so worried. And Tania's always been more of a kisser than a hugger."

I think back on it. She definitely initiated the kiss, and he didn't exactly throw his arms around her and lock her against the wall. My body sags, thinking of that night. "I'm so sorry about Jo. She was a wonder."

"She was." He swipes something invisible off the counter. "She liked you a lot, you know. Thank you for coming to the funeral."

Doug's sitting between us now, his head swiveling as we speak. His wrinkles always give him a worried look, but he seems extra concerned right now.

"I've wanted to see you, Amelia. But things have been really hard the last few weeks. And I wasn't sure what to say. Your messages didn't explain much about why Tim was there. After I saw you with him, I figured things between you had changed. I thought you wanted to say good-bye, and I've had enough of that recently."

I move a step closer. "Tim came back because I told him I didn't want to talk to him anymore, and that Doug needed a break. He came back, I think, because he knew he was losing us. He wants to get back together."

Travis body tenses. "And what did you say?"

"I emailed him and told him no. Tim and I are definitely over."

A smile lifts his lips as he closes the distance between us by another step. Doug growls and scoots back toward me too.

"Does this mean you're ready to see other people?"

I nod. "Certain other people. If they're ready, too."

He reaches for my hands. Doug whines, his butt up against my ankles now, trapped between us.

Travis studies my face. "Are you sure this is what you want, Amelia? I mean, *I* knew you were special the minute I met you. The way you apologized a thousand times after Doug tackled me in the parking lot. How worried you were about him. The way you spoke to Jo. You were kind to Brenda, and great with my patients. Every day I spent with you, I wanted more. And then, after we kissed—" He touches both sides of his head and open his fingers in a mind-blown gesture. "When I saw you with Tim . . . I just couldn't handle it. Not after Tania. Between you and Jo, I've been a mess."

"I wish you'd let me explain sooner."

"I was an idiot. Do you forgive me?" His eyes fall to my lips. He's tantalizingly close, but I have one more question.

"What about the invoice you sent? No note, no nothing with it? Of course I want to pay Doug's bill, but it seemed like you were saying you were done with us."

His eyebrows pinch together. "Invoice? I didn't send any invoices. I've barely managed to see my patients. If Jo and you hadn't worked so hard to pull the party together, I would have canceled it."

"I can show you the email."

He shakes his head, then he groans. "Jo. She was working on setting up an automated billing system. I forgot about that. Amelia —I'd never just cut Doug off without a plan. Sounds like I screwed up a bunch of things the last few weeks."

I smile and grab on to the V of his scrub shirt to pull him close. "Then . . . I guess that makes us perfect for each other."

Nudging Doug out of the way, I wrap my arms around Travis. Our lips meet, and I never want to let him go again.

From beside us, Doug howls, a sound of pure betrayal and heartbreak. Startled, I pull away to look at him. Someone knocks at the door, then opens it. Kenny pokes his head in.

"Hello? Dr. Brewer?" His eyes go wide when he sees us. "Oh. I'm sorry to interrupt."

Leash trailing, Doug bolts past Kenny and escapes through the door.

Chapter Twenty-Seven

✿

"Doug, no!"

I tear by Kenny, Ruston, and Kenny's mom, who jumps back, clutching Chi-Chi against her.

"He went that way!" Ruston points a chocolate ice-cream cone to my right.

With Travis behind me, I race in that direction. Scanning the crowd, I catch sight of Avery's blond hair. She looks mystified.

"Doug!" I yell.

"We're coming!" She drops a drink in the trash and starts to follow, Jason with her. Have I mentioned I love them? Even Brenda, the ears of her pug suit flopping, scans the park for Doug.

His curly tail is ahead of me, leash bouncing behind. He sprints across the street, taking my breath away as a car swerves then brakes so as not to hit him, and he disappears around a corner.

Adrenaline shoots through me. Doug is not an off-leash kind of dog. He has no experience with being alone around cars. I put on speed, grateful I wore sneakers today and hit the treadmill at the gym a few times this month.

I shout at him again. Avery and Jason call to him as well. I shoot a look back; Kenny and Ruston have joined in the chase.

Tearing around the corner, I search the street. A white sedan drives toward me, and a black SUV heads the other way. A couple walk, heads together, toward me.

"Did you see . . . a pug run by?" I ask.

They shake their heads. "No, sorry."

I fly to the end of the street. Nothing. Frantic, I whirl around. In every direction is another street, sets of condos, rows of restaurants and businesses. There's very little green space where he might be safe and plenty of places for him to hide.

He's microchipped and wearing his collar, but they both have Tim's name and old contact information, not mine.

Jason catches up to me. "Which way did he go?"

I put my hands on my head. "I don't know!"

Avery stops beside us and rests on her knees. "I need . . . to exercise . . . more."

Kenny and Ruston come in, followed by a tween girl and an older man with a bounding black lab who must have heard what was happening and followed. I straighten up. This area is too big to search randomly. Time to coordinate.

I point to the left. "Jason, you and Avery search that way. You —" I point to the girl and older man, "please head down that street straight ahead. Kenny and Ruston, look in that alley across the street. I'll go to the park in case he doubles back that way. If anyone finds him, bring him there." I glance around. "Where's Travis?"

The tween raises her hand like she's in school. "You mean Dr. Travis?"

"Yes." I try not to sound impatient.

"I passed him running. He turned around and went back to the park."

I thank her and the man, and we all take off. As more people jog up to help, some with their dogs on leashes, Avery gives them another direction to search.

I run back to the park, head swiveling, my mouth dry and

hands cold. Music continues to thump out of several speakers. Some kind of classic rock song. I'm looking for Travis as well as Doug now. Why did he come back?

I spot Travis in the small covered gazebo at the center of the park, where the sound system is set up. He's talking to the DJ. What is he doing?

The classic rock fades out in the middle of the song, and a new beat takes its place, a very familiar one. A smile breaks over my face. *Travis, you're a genius!*

"Girl, I love you so bad, your love, it drives me mad . . ." pours out of the speakers, flowing through the park and into the surrounding streets as the DJ turns up the volume. Lil' Dougie never sounded so good.

As I reach the gazebo, Jason's deep voice booms over the music. "Here he comes!"

I turn that way. People part on either side of the sidewalk, jumping back, surprise and amusement on their faces. One guy's drink goes flying as he stumbles out of the way. A child screeches and grabs her mother's legs. I peer down the path.

Ears flapping, tail up, short legs moving so fast they're a blur, Doug sprints this way, searching for the source of the music.

Looking for Tim.

What will he do when he sees Travis instead?

My dog almost tumbles heels over head as he stops. Muzzle askew on his face, chest heaving, he eyes Travis. Avery, Jason, Kenny, Ruston, and the others jog up. The crowd, all kinds of pets and their owners, gather around.

A long moment passes. Then Travis crouches, arms out, and calls to Doug. I hold my breath.

Unbelievably, Doug leaps into his arms, knocking him over *again*, this time trying to lick his face. Travis pulls the muzzle off so he can.

Avery and I turn to each other, eyes wide, then throw our arms around each other. She only lets go when Travis carries Doug to me. With him snuggled between us, Travis kisses me gently.

"You *must* be Dr. Travis," Kenny says from behind me. "I've heard a lot about you." Laughing I introduce everyone. Travis thanks Kenny and Ruston for coming, and Kenny's mama and Chi-Chi, too. Chi-Chi's whole body quivers, and he can't stop yapping with excitement.

"Amelia," Ruston asks. "Whatever happened with that awful Max person and his threats?"

I shake my head. "You know, I'm not sure. He said he would call animal control about Doug attacking him, but they still haven't contacted me."

Ruston grins and fist bumps Kenny.

"What?" I ask, smiling.

Kenny smirks. "I got his email you forwarded while we were in PV. I *might* have had a word with Jim. Asked him to tell Max to back off. I know a thing or two about the practice's finances that Hart, Hand, and Butz probably don't want anyone else to know. A little blackmail for a good cause never hurts." He winks at me, solemn, like an owl.

I put Doug down and embrace my friend. "Kenny, I love you. Thank you so much."

"Love you, too, Princess."

Doug jerks me away from Kenny and drags me to greet Brenda and Daisy.

"Well. Are you ready for the newest member of your family?" Brenda holds Daisy's leash out to Travis with one paw of her pug suit. The dogs touch noses with curly tails wagging wildly.

I cover my mouth and stare at him. "*You're* adopting Daisy?"

Travis shrugs and smiles. "Brenda told me she hadn't found a family for Daisy yet. She has so much spunk and independence, adopting her seems like a good way to honor Jo's memory." He steps closer. "I thought Doug and Daisy might like to spend more time together. Get to know each other better. I'm hoping you'd like to come along."

I wrap myself around him, and we share the first of many completely perfect kisses.

Travis and I are pet people. Lucky for us, sometimes that brings more than half-eaten underwear and carpet stains.

Sometimes, it brings true love.

Epilogue

Travis pulls the shoulder of my brand-new pink scrub top over a little and kisses my neck. Goose bumps shoot down my arms. His voice in my ear and his gentle touch still turn my legs to jelly.

"Ready for your first patients?" he asks.

When I nod, he walks to the door of the RV and hops out to help Brenda carry in a box full of squirming pug puppies.

All black, with googly eyes, tiny needle teeth, and chubby bellies, each puglet is small enough to fit in a coffee mug. I can't help oohing at them.

"Congratulations on your internship, Amelia," she says. "I know Dr. Travis will enjoy having you on board."

"I will. And I need the help since Jo . . ." Even two years later, pain crosses his face. I touch his arm. "Let's just say I've needed Amelia in more ways than one."

We smile, our eyes lingering on each other.

Soon after the first annual Love & Pets Party, I gave notice at HHB and signed up for a veterinary-technician training program. After Kenny left for law school, quitting was a no brainer.

Tim was unhappy about my break-up email. But I knew I'd made the right choice when I saw his reaction to my suggestion that I keep Doug full time and allow him visitation. His head practically exploded over Skype. He never would have been that upset about losing me.

After some negotiation, we decided that I'd keep Doug during the week and he could have him on weekends. Since Global Ballers took off, and Tim began to travel more to set it up, the pug co-parenting arrangement has been working pretty well.

To pay for my program, I got a job part-time as a barista and helped Travis with streamlining his scheduling, billing, and book-keeping using the systems I learned at HHB. I completed my program's class work a few weeks ago, and I'm starting my practical internship today.

Best of all, when I graduate in three months, I'll have a job lined up in the Love & Pets Mobile Animal Clinic with Travis—my business partner and soon-to-be husband. The wedding will be next summer.

Brenda clears her throat. "Well. Should we get these puglets immunized?"

The oval-shaped diamond on my finally not-so-naked hand sparkles in the sun as I reach for the first puppy. "I wish Doug and Daisy were here to see these guys."

"How are those love pugs?" Brenda asks.

I smile at Travis, who grins back.

"Perfect together."

THE END

It all started with a girl, a boy, and a pug named Doug.
Get the exclusive Love & Pets prequel for FREE!

Love & Pets Box Set: Books 1 - 3
Read The Problem with Pugs, The Trouble with Tabbies, and The Downside of Dachshunds in one convenient box set!

Read Love & Pets Book 2
Her cats are here to stay. But is he?
Buy The Trouble with Tabbies!

Read Next

The Trouble with Tabbies: Love & Pets #2

Chapter One

Beatrix

I swing my Range Rover into one of the last available parking spaces outside the Thirsty Lion Brewery and turn off the engine. A soft meow comes from the back seat.

I turn and smile into the bright green eyes of Fluffernutter, my tiny tuxedo cat who's peering out of the soft-sided carrier I'd strapped in with the seat belt.

"Ready?" I ask.

Fluff meows again, which I interpret as a yes. I get out, unbuckle the carrier, take the last in a long series of deep, settling breaths, and enter the fray.

Most days, the Thirsty Lion is a low-key craft brewery in Evergreen, a small town in the foothills west of Denver, Colorado. People come here to hike, bike, fish, or to enjoy a pint and the scenery on a sweet, summery afternoon.

But one Saturday in July every year, the Thirsty Lion hosts Colorado Cat Rescue's big annual event: Colorado Adopts Cats, a fund raiser and cat adoption event. Today's that day. People sit at tables with beers, listening to music, while others cruise the shade tents nearby that offer everything from cat toys to locally produced cat food.

I beeline toward CCR's large tent set up in the center of the event, scratching one arm and then the other as I walk. I feel my face redden, and I haven't even had to speak to anyone yet. Some people are allergic to cats. Not me. People give me hives.

I enter the tent, and the sight of all those cats in cages focuses me. Big and small, short and long haired, monochrome or with distinctive markings, the cats and kittens prowl, prance, and tumble around the enclosures like living fur balls. They're every imaginable combination of breeds, from the common American shorthair to a rare Manx with its unusually short tail.

I lift Fluff up in her carrier so she can see and hear all the cats better. She stares unblinking at the mass of felines, her tail twitching like she's found a bird, squirrel, and mouse hot-tubbing together in her water bowl.

People walk among the cages, pointing and smiling at various cats. Families, couples, singles—they're all here to adopt rescue cats. I push my glasses up my nose and swipe the tear of happiness that leaks out of one eye.

"Beatrix! You made it!" Vilma, a middle-aged Latina with a bright green event t-shirt, ankle-length patterned maxi skirt, and closed-toed hiking sandals waves me over to a table at the center of the tent. It's covered in pamphlets about CCR, stuffed cats for purchase to support the nonprofit, and sample bags of cat food.

"Ooh, I love your shirt!" she says.

I glance down to remind myself what I'm wearing; it's my *I didn't choose the cat lady life, the cat lady life chose me* tee today.

"And *hola* to you, too, *dulzura*." Vilma, CCR's executive director, coos at Fluff through the carrier gate. She'd met Fluff several times when I'd brought her to board meetings. She probably thinks I'm a kook for toting an emotional support cat everywhere I go, but she's always welcomed us.

"Looks like you have a good turnout," I say.

She puffs out a breath and pushes her wiry gray-brown hair out of her face. "It's been a lot of work to pull together, like every year. But Bea," she clutches my hand in hers, "we could not have done this without your financial support. I wish you would let me acknowledge you in our materials or on the website."

I cradle Fluff and her carrier under my free arm and look around at the milling people smiling and laughing at the antics of all the cats. "It's enough to know that so many of these fur babies will have homes after today. And that we'll get the permanent adoption center built soon."

Vilma hands a brochure to a man browsing the table beside me. "Thank you for supporting the homeless cats of Colorado." When he moves away, she turns back to me. "After we recover from this weekend, we'll set up a board meeting for planning. Maybe in early September?"

"Perfect," I say, but unease shoots through me. I'd promised Vilma I'd help pay for the center. The problem is, I don't have the money yet.

I love cats—a lot. I've rescued dozens myself, and I support CCR as much as I can with my own income writing romance books, but this is an expensive project. I need my portion of the money from our family trust, my inheritance, which my father has promised to give me . . . soon.

A harried-looking man with thinning white hair and wearing the same green shirt as Vilma rushes over to us.

"Vilma, sweetpea, I think one of the kittens needs medical help. She's thrown up a few times and is looking peaky. Oh, hello, Bea, so good to see you." Robert, Vilma's husband and another member of the CCR board, shakes my free hand. His smile is yellow, crooked, and radiant. "We're getting incredible interest in the event; Channel 9 is stopping by to film soon for the five o'clock news."

"That's wonderful," I say. "You're doing great work."

"And you, Bea. You are, too." Vilma beams at me, then turns to Robert, all business. "Dr. Travis is outside. Take the sick *gatita* to him. He said he'd squeeze in any of our cats that need to be seen between his scheduled patients."

"Dr. Travis is here?" I ask.

Vilma smiles. "You know him?" She presses her hands to her chest. "Such a kind man."

"He's my veterinarian . . . I mean my cats' veterinarian." *Duh, Bea.* "I can take the sick kitten out to him."

Vilma looks grateful, and distracted, as another green-shirted volunteer calls to her from a nearby cage where a family seems to have chosen a sweet ragdoll to adopt. "*Gracias*, Beatrix, that would be so helpful."

Robert leads me to a cage sitting by itself along the side of the tent. "She's over here in the makeshift infirmary. I'll be back in a snap with a cat carrier."

A tiny gray Russian blue cat hunches in a corner of the cage. I can tell at a glance that the kitten isn't well. Her ears are down, and she's panting. Poor thing.

"What do you think is wrong with her, Fluff?" I ask my cat in a low voice. I don't actually expect her to respond. I'm not *that* much of a cat lady. Good thing, too, because she doesn't.

The sickly kitten doesn't even look our way. My heart double thumps. I can't stand to see any animal suffer. Robert returns, reaches into the cage, gently scoops up the kitten, and places her in the carrier. She doesn't resist.

He hands her over and flashes his toothy grin before he walks away. "Thank you again, Beatrix. I'm back to the trenches."

I tell him goodbye and, a carrier in each hand, hurry outside to find Travis Brewer, DVM. How did I miss him on the way in? I must be more anxious than I thought. I squint, searching the grounds.

There it is. The bright blue-green recreational vehicle with the Love & Pets Mobile Animal Clinic logo painted on the side is parked in a corner of the Thirsty Lion's lot. As I approach, I spot a sign on the door asking people to wait. The staff is with a patient.

I settle on a nearby bench, cat carriers on both sides, and pull out my phone to pass the time. I check my social media pages quickly, responding apologetically to a few disappointed comments about the delay of the release of my next book. Trust me, no one's more disappointed in the delay than me. Then, I open Gmail. Hearing from readers makes my day. Who am I kidding? It makes my month.

Instead, an email from my older sister, Aggie, waits unopened at the top of my email pile. With a familiar panicky jolt in my stomach, I click on it.

Beatrix, she begins. She never calls me by my nickname, Bea. And she hates that I still use her childhood nickname, Aggie. "It's *Agatha*, Beatrix," she says every time.

I'm hosting an 80th birthday party for Father. Family only. He wants you to come and to bring your boyfriend. And he wants to discuss your inheritance.

Although I knew this day would come, my hands shake and my heart pounds.

Aggie gave the date of the party, three weeks away, at the end of the email. I shove the phone back in my pocket, the cheerful sounds of the event suddenly muffled.

Not going home to Aspen isn't an option. I can tell from Aggie's tone that Dad ordered me to be there. In our family, that's like an emailed summons from God. Which means very soon Dad, my three older siblings—Aggie, Thomas, and Henry—and their spouses will inspect and judge me, and I'll be found wanting. Well, not Henry so much, but the others for sure.

And the panic-inducing prospect of spending time with my family is only part of the trouble. The real problem is that I have to bring my boyfriend.

A boyfriend . . . that doesn't exist.

Read The Trouble with Tabbies (Love & Pets 2)

Acknowledgments

This was such a fun book to write. What's not to like about love and pets? For me, they've always gone hand in hand. That said, every book I've written has had its own set of challenges, and a unique group of helpers and cheerleaders I've relied on while the work got done. This one was no exception.

First, I owe an enormous debt of gratitude to Laura Perkins, my good friend and an amazing publishing assistant. Anything I asked for, she provided with good humor, generosity, and professionalism. Laura, as I've told you many times, I could not have survived the last six months without you. Thank you!

I'd also like to thank my editor, Maya Myers. If you need a developmental or copyedit completed with speed and accuracy, she's your woman. Thank you to Jen Weston, DVM for answering my questions as I wrote an earlier draft of this book, when instead of a pug, Amelia owned a pet prairie dog. (Don't ask.)

My author friends Rebecca Taylor, Kristi Helvig, and Shawn McGuire provided much needed writing and publishing advice and emotional support as I wrote. Thank you always, ladies.

Rebecca deserves a special shoutout for suggesting I change my prairie dog to the canine variety. (I told you not to ask!) And I'm grateful to her son Matthew Taylor for lending me his precious pug, Bella, for a delightful afternoon of pug research.

Finally, thank you to my family. Your love and support provide me the inspiration, motivation, and dedication to continue writing. I love you all.

Also by A. G. Henley

The Love & Pets Series (Sweet Romantic Comedy)

Love, Pugs, and Other Problems: A Love & Pets Prequel Story

The Problem with Pugs

The Trouble with Tabbies

The Downside of Dachshunds

The Lessons of Labradors

The Predicament of Persians

The Conundrum of Collies

The Pandemonium of Pets: A Love & Pets Christmas Romance

The Love & Pets Series Box Set: Books 1 - 3

Nicole Rossi Thrillers (Young Adult)

Double Black Diamond

The Brilliant Darkness Series (Young Adult Fantasy)

The Scourge

The Keeper: A Brilliant Darkness Story

The Defiance

The Gatherer: A Brilliant Darkness Story

The Fire Sisters

The Brilliant Darkness Boxed Set

Novellas (Young Adult Fantasy)

Untimely

Featured in *Tick Tock: Seven Tales of Time*

Basil and Jade

Featured in *Off Beat: Nine Spins on Song*

The Escape Room

Featured in *Dead Night: Four Fits of Fear*

About the Author

A.G. Henley is a *USA Today* bestselling author of novels and stories in multiple genres including thrillers, romantic comedies, and fantasy romances. The first book in her young adult Brilliant Darkness series, *The Scourge*, was a Library Journal Self-e Selection and a Next Generation Indie Book Award finalist. She's also a clinical psychologist, but she promises not to analyze you . . . much.

Find her at:
aghenley.com
Email Aimee

www.ingramcontent.com/pod-product-compliance
Lightning Source LLC
Chambersburg PA
CBHW032144170626
46808CB00006B/2360